Lips Touch

THREE TIMES

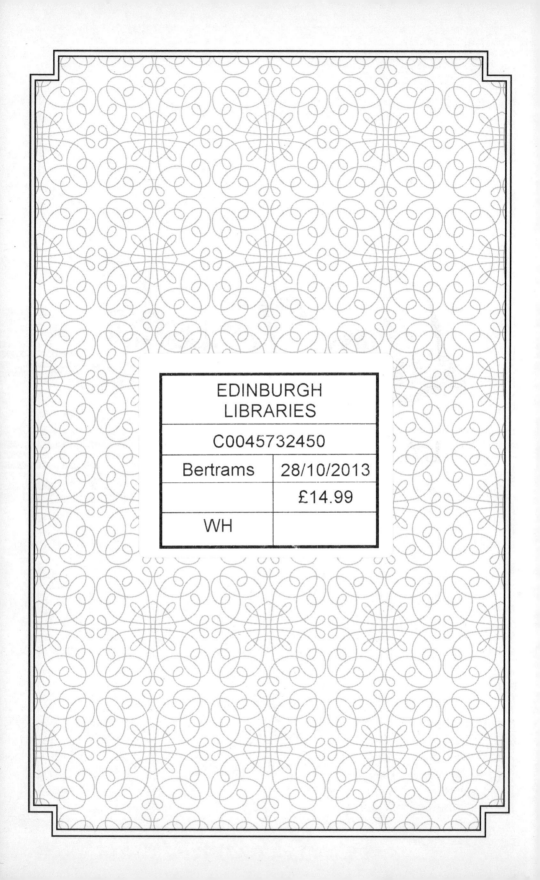

THREE TIMES

LAINI TAYLOR

With Illustrations By **JIM DI BARTOLO**

H
HODDER &
STOUGHTON

First published in the United States of America in 2009
by Arthur A. Levine Books
An imprint of Scholastic Inc.

First published in Great Britain in 2013 by Hodder & Stoughton
An Hachette UK company

'Goblin Fruit' and 'Spicy Little Curses Such as These'
first published in Great Britain in 2012 as eBook-only short stories
by Hodder & Stoughton

1

Text copyright © 2009 Laini Taylor
Illustrations copyright © 2009 Jim Di Bartolo

A CIP catalogue record for this title is available from the British Library.

Hardback ISBN 978 1 444 73150 7
eBook ISBN 978 1 444 73152 1

Printed and bound by Clays Ltd, St Ives plc

Hodder & Stoughton policy is to use papers that are natural, renewable and
recyclable products and made from wood grown in sustainable forests. The
logging and manufacturing processes are expected to conform to the
environmental regulations of the country of origin.

Hodder & Stoughton Ltd
338 Euston Road
London NW1 3BH

www.hodder.co.uk

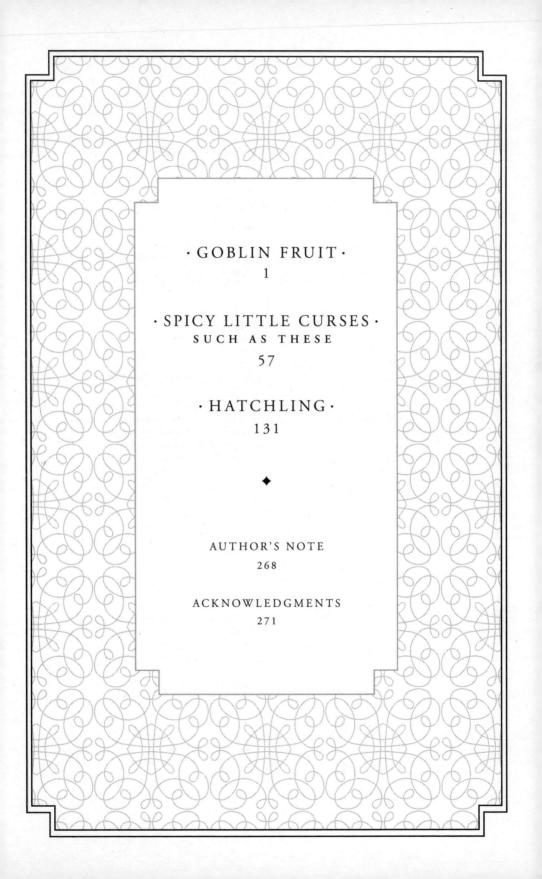

Soul meets soul on lovers' lips.

PERCY BYSSHE SHELLEY
Prometheus Unbound

*For Christina Rossetti, the British Raj,
and Zarathustra, and for Jim,
who pesters gently.*

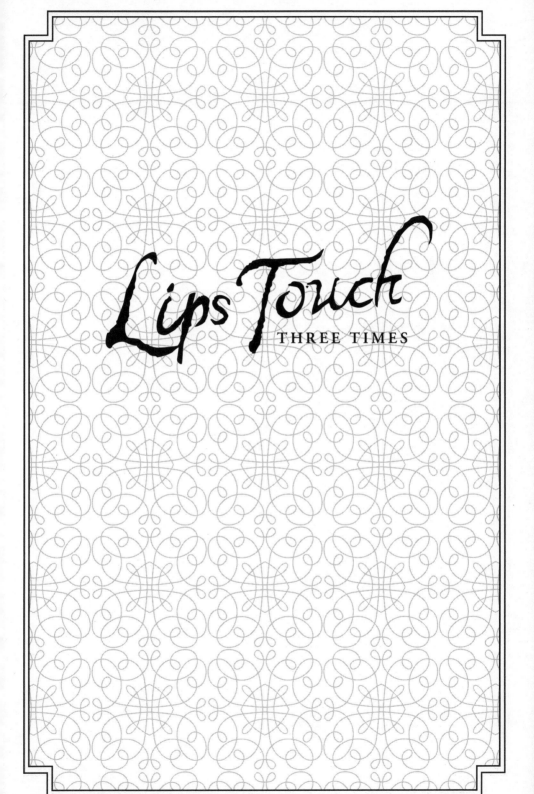

Lips Touch

THREE TIMES

· GOBLIN FRUIT ·

· GOBLIN FRUIT ·

There is a certain kind of girl the goblins crave. You could walk across a high school campus and point them out: not her, not her, *her*. The pert, lovely ones with butterfly tattoos in secret places, sitting on their boyfriends' laps? No, not them. The girls *watching* the lovely ones sitting on their boyfriends' laps? Yes.

Them.

The goblins want girls who dream so hard about being pretty their yearning leaves a palpable trail, a scent goblins can follow like sharks on a soft bloom of blood. The girls with hungry eyes who pray each night to wake up as someone else. Urgent, unkissed, wishful girls.

Like Kizzy.

Fierce with Wanting

Kizzy's family lived in the weird house outside of town with all the anvils in the yard and the tick-ridden billy goat that rammed the fence whenever anyone walked past. The mailman wouldn't come up to the door, which worked out fine, since no one ever wrote to them. They didn't even get credit card offers and junk mail like normal people did.

Kizzy's family wasn't normal.

They had no TV but knew hundreds of songs – all of them in a language that Kizzy's teachers had never even heard of – and they sat on rickety chairs in the yard and sang them together, their voices as plaintive as wolves', howling at the moon. There were a lot of hairy, blue-eyed uncles strumming old, beautiful guitars, and stout aunts who dried flowers to smoke in their pipes. Cousins were numerous. Small and swift, they were always aswirl in the women's skirts or dodging the goat like wee shrill matadors. Kizzy's mother wore a kerchief like she was some peasant in a foreign film, and her father had lost two fingers to a wolf back in the Old Country. He'd killed it to get his fingers back and he kept the little bones in a pouch around his neck, along with the teeth of the very same wolf who'd swallowed them.

The women of the family were in charge of the garden, and the men hunted whatever was in season (or wasn't). They did things in their scattered, crooked sheds that most suburban kids would only ever see in a documentary, or perhaps on a church mission to a third-world country – things involving axes and offal and an intimate understanding of how to turn an *animal* into a *meal*.

Kizzy hated it all, and she kind of hated herself too, by association. She hated mirrors, hated her ankles, hated her hair. She wanted to climb out of her life as if it were a seashell she could abandon on a shore and walk away from, barefoot. No one else on the whole landmass of North America, she was sure, had such a stupid life.

Besides the anvils and the goat, there were plenty of no-name cats in the yard, always slinking and slipping along the edges of things, and there were chickens, a peacock that screamed *'rape!'* (as peacocks do), and some cars on blocks. Ghosts came from miles around to whisper and mope and feed, and sometimes strangers passed through in big, battered cars filled with all the things they owned and stayed a few days, playing accordions, swigging moonshine, and singing ballads whose words had never known paper but lived only on the rasping edge of their own voices. Kizzy liked the ghosts but not the strangers, because her father made her give up her room for them and they always left it smelling like feet.

She was sixteen, smart but unenthusiastic, a junior at a public high school she referred to as Saint Pock Mark's Finishing School for Cannibals.

Saint Pock Mark was her nickname for the acne-scarred principal who used any pretext to talk about his time among the cannibals as a missionary in Borneo, where as a younger man he had suffered parasites and bodily mildew in the service of the Lord. His thin lips got even thinner whenever Kizzy was brought to his office for skipping school, and she took a wicked pleasure in inventing imaginary religious holidays to explain her absences. She knew he'd sooner grit his teeth and accept her stories than call her parents, who yelled on the phone as if it were a futuristic device, and whose loud exclamations in their own language Kizzy had half convinced him were gypsy curses.

Even more than most teenagers, Kizzy hated to be seen in public with any member of her family, and she chose to walk to school even in the sleet or the rare skimpy snows. Freezing was preferable to the rusting junk-heap cars and belly-scratching uncles. She was deeply susceptible to mortification: easy to embarrass though hard to disgust. At home she did unsavory chores that ought to have gone extinct with the old days, like rendering lard and chopping the heads off chickens.

She drank too much coffee, smoked, had a thrilling singing voice when she could be persuaded to use it, and was saddled with a terrible nickname at school that she feared would follow her through life. She had two friends: Evie, who was fat, and Cactus, who was sarcastic and whose name wasn't really Cactus, but Mary.

'Shut up, Kizzy. You have *not* chopped the head off a swan,' Evie declared as the girls walked home from school on a Friday, smoking.

'Um. *Yes.* I have,' Kizzy replied. 'We needed one of its wings to put in my nana's coffin.'

'Uh! Guh! *Horrible!*'

'Please. That swan was a total bastard.'

'But you cut off its head? That's totally cruel.'

'Cruel? I cut off chickens' heads all the time. It's not cruel. It's, like, *food*, Evie. You do know food isn't born wrapped in plastic, right?'

'You *ate* it? I am so telling Mick Crespain you're a swan-eater.'

'I didn't eat it! And I'm sure you'd walk up to Mick Crespain and start telling him about my eating habits. He'd be like, *Um, who are you?*'

'No, he'd be like, *Um, what's a kizzy?*'

'He knows my name! I sit right behind him in Trig. I've totally memorized the back of his neck. I could pick him out of a neck lineup.'

Cactus had been silently exhaling long plumes of smoke but she interrupted now and said, 'Hell with Crespain's neck. What I want to know is, why would you put a swan's wing in your grandmother's coffin?'

Kizzy replied as if the answer was obvious. 'So her soul could fly. *Duh.*'

Cactus laughed and choked on smoke. 'So what'd you do with the other wing?'

'We're saving it for whoever dies next,' said Kizzy, laughing too. 'Swan wings don't grow on trees, you know. Or,' she added, with a glance at Evie, 'maybe you *don't* know.'

'Maybe I don't *care.*'

Cactus was still coughing. She managed to say, 'God, Kizzy. If I had your freak-ass family I'd totally get an eye patch and write pathetic books about my childhood and go on *Oprah* to tell about how I had to behead a swan so I could put its wing in my grandmother's coffin.'

'So her soul could fly,' added Evie.

'*Obviously.*'

'Shut up!' Kizzy said, swatting at them halfheartedly with her fists. 'Cactus, you can *have* my family. Take them all. Just give me your tiny little mother with her tiny little haircut and your snoring-ass dad on the couch, and nothing to behead ever again. I bequeath you my axe.'

'Thank you. I accept your offer of weaponry,' Cactus said formally. 'I doubt I could kill a swan, though. Even a big bastard one. I just don't have your rage, Kiz.'

'Believe me, if you had my family, you'd have my rage. You know what my dad did last night? He was cleaning an elk carcass in the yard and he came in and stuck his big bloody hand right in my popcorn bowl!'

Evie and Cactus both shrieked in disgust. 'Okay, I take it back,' Cactus said with a grimace. 'You can keep your family.'

'What, over a little bloody popcorn?' asked Kizzy. Shaking her head, she muttered, '*Wuss.*'

The girls parted ways at the edge of the normal houses and Kizzy kept walking into the straggling edge of the countryside, past a cemetery, a water tower, and a Christmas tree farm with a little trailer near the road, where a fat dog lying on the porch picked up his head and belched as she passed. A gutsy little bird chased a crow out of a tree, and a squirrel miscalculated his leap and fell stunned into a pile of rotting leaves. It was autumn. The sky was white and the trees black. Kizzy saw herself in a puddle and looked away.

The goblins didn't look away. Their mouths filled up with saliva as they watched her. There was scant cover for them in the leafless hawthorns along the main road, and Kizzy should have seen them. Of all the girls in this unremarkable town, she should have been the one they couldn't get, the one who knew better. She had Old World blood, after all. Her family *believed in things*: in vampires and the evil eye, in witch soldiers and curses and even talking foxes. They believed that black roosters are the devil in costume and that fruit grown out of season should never be trusted or tasted.

And of course they believed in goblins.

They'd have said there was no 'believing' involved. They *knew*, because Kizzy's grandmother had saved her sister from them once in the Old Country and lived to tell. She'd never tired of telling the story, how the goblins had tried to force her mouth open and cram in their unnatural fruit, how she'd kept her jaw clamped tight against them.

How swollen her lips had been after.

'As bruised as windfall plums! I could smell that sweet nectar all over my skin but I never tasted it,' she had told Kizzy many times. 'You never want to taste their fruit, Sunshine.'

'It's not like there are goblins *here*, Nana,' Kizzy had replied one time, bored of the story, and bored of this town with its soulless mall and soccer fields, its houses all alike as cookies in a bakery box. 'Goblins probably get to live in Prague and Barcelona where they have, like, coffeehouses and absinthe and . . .' She trailed off, groping through her daydreams for the many coveted things to be had in other cities, in other people's better lives. 'Blind street musicians' was what she came up with. 'And mean little nuns carrying long bread under their arms. And cathedrals with gargoyles. And catacombs.'

'You know so much?' her grandmother had chuffed at her. 'Goblins living in Prague? Silly girl! Goblins live in Hell! I need to tell you that? They only come *here* to hunt.'

If Kizzy's grandmother were alive, she would have seen the goblins crouched behind the trees. She would have heard the *smack* and *gluck* of their juicy mouths and kept Kizzy safe. But she wasn't alive. She had gone into the unknowable last summer. Besides the swan's wing, they'd buried her with other things she'd need: her pockets full of almonds to eat, a compass for finding her path, and coins for bribes along the way – silver coins, minted in one of the sheds and inscribed with runes. And of course, the dainty stiletto blade she'd always carried in her pocket – that went into her coffin too.

When Kizzy was a little girl, she had asked once if she could have that knife when her grandmother died, and her grandmother had answered, 'Sunshine, I'll need it where I'm going. Get your own damn knife.'

Kizzy knew other families didn't bury their grandmothers with knives and dried-out swan wings, and she suspected other grandmothers didn't slip out of their graves to dance deasil round the living either – that meant circling clockwise and it was powerful magic, especially when the dead did it. Kizzy had felt her grandmother's ghost go thrice around her at the graveside as her father and uncles shoveled dirt clods onto her coffin. She'd been glad to know her soul wasn't down there where the rain of dirt must have sounded like thunder. The knife was, though; she'd seen her father put it in and she'd mourned it. She had never stopped coveting it with its sweet mother-of-pearl handle, and her grandmother must have known because on her deathbed she'd motioned Kizzy close and whispered, 'Remember my knife, Sunshine?'

Kizzy had thought she was going to give it to her and she'd nodded, smiling. But the old lady had whispered, 'Don't you dare steal it out of my coffin,' and then she'd died.

Sometimes Kizzy imagined her grandmother knife-fighting her way down the long tunnel of death, but mostly her daydreams were of a very different nature. She daydreamed of slow-dancing with Mick Crespain and of sitting on his lap at lunch while he hugged *her* around the waist instead of Sarah Ferris, his knuckles resting lightly against the underside of *her* breasts instead of Sarah's. She daydreamed about having slim ankles like Jenny Glass instead of peasant ankles like the fetlocks of a draft horse. About smooth hair instead of coarse hair, sleek hips instead of belly dancer's hips. About a tinkling laugh, and a butterfly tattoo, and a boy who would tuck his hand into her back jeans pocket while they walked, and press her up against a fence to suck her lower lip like a globe of fruit.

Kizzy wanted it all so bad her soul leaned half out of her body hungering after it, and that was what drove the goblins wild, her soul hanging out there like an untucked shirt. No amount of grandmother-ghosts dancing deasil would keep them from trying for so raw a soul. They just wanted her that bad. She'd probably have been flattered to learn someone wanted her so much, even if that someone was a goblin.

'Some of the goblins have tails and whiskers,' went her grandmother's story. 'Antlers and snail shells and gills. Hooves, claws, beaks! Creatures, they are, each as different from the next as God's creatures in a zoo – but they aren't God's! They work for Old Scratch and catch his souls for him, and they almost had my sister's. She was ready to give it for just one more taste of their fruit.

'She was a lot like you, Sunshine. Mairenni was always fierce with wanting something, a new scarf or our brother's guitar or a wink from the handsome blacksmith. And when the goblin men came through the glen, calling out soft like doves cooing, "Come

21

buy our orchard fruits, come buy!" she wanted that too and she had it, handfuls and mouthfuls of that witched fruit. Pears, pomegranates, dates, figs. And the pineapples! We'd never seen pineapples before. Mairenni was a fool to trust their fruit – where in our mountains did she think such things grew?

'She said it was sweeter than honey and richer than wine, and maybe it was, but it near carved her hollow – because it's all she wanted after and all she thought of, day after day, like it was a drug that shrank her mind to a little nub of *want*, and she wanted and wanted and wanted after it, but she couldn't have any more.

'She haunted that glen looking for the goblin men, but she couldn't see them, even when they were there! I could hear their cooing, coaxing voices and see their ugly shadows tramping up the hill, and so could our cousin Peneli, but not Mairenni. It's how they do it, torment a girl with wanting and lure out her soul like a snail from its shell, until she can barely feel it anymore and it seems like a skimpy, worthless thing to trade away.

'A girl from the next village had died already. Wasted away. I saw her near the end. Her eyes were huge in her face and all the juice looked wrung out of her. She died on the full moon and they buried her in the churchyard, but they dug her back out the next year because nothing would grow by her grave, not even grass, and that's how they knew she was damned. Mairenni started to look like that poor girl and I knew she'd die too. She was my sister even if she was a fool. I had to do something.'

At this point in the story Kizzy's grandmother used to shiver over her memories and touch her lips, remembering how the crowd of goblins had turned on her, their creature eyes flashing in the gloom as they jumped on her and held her down, mashing grapes and figs against her prim, clenched mouth.

'The goblins can't just *take* your soul, Sunshine,' she had said in her thick accent. 'You have to *give* it. It's an old agreement between God and Old Scratch. Older than eggs! A soul that's taken unwilling spoils like milk and then it's no good to anyone, not even Old Scratch. That's why he grows his evil orchards, because once you've tasted his fruit you'll give anything to taste it again, and there's only one thing he wants.'

Mairenni had been ready to give up that one thing. But instead, her sister had braved the goblins and come home bruised and bleeding, with the pulp of that evil fruit still sticky on her skin, and Mairenni, wasted and white, had clung to her and wept. She had kissed her and tasted the juice on her skin – the juice she was supposed to give her soul for, sipped for free from her sister's skin – and the spell had been broken. Mairenni had lived.

Kizzy had never met her – Mairenni had stayed behind in the Old Country – but her grandmother said she looked like her. There was a single sepia photograph of a girl in a doorway, full-lipped, with eyes that seemed to sparkle with secrets. Kizzy had always been fascinated by her – truth be told, she had always identified more with that wild girl who almost sold her soul for the taste of figs than with her grandmother who kept her lips tight shut and never hungered for forbidden things. But though she stared at that photo, and even saw the shape of her own eyes and lips mirrored back at her, Kizzy just couldn't see herself in that long-ago girl, ripe and thrilling and flush with a weird species of beauty the young have no vocabulary for.

Kizzy was so busy wishing she was Sarah Ferris or Jenny Glass that she could scarcely see herself at all, and she was certainly blind to her own weird beauty: her heavy, spell-casting eyes, too-wide mouth, wild hair, and hips that could be wild too, if they learned how. No one else in town looked anything like her, and if she lived to womanhood, she was the one artists would want to draw, not the Sarahs and Jennys. She was the one who would some day know a dozen ways to wear a silk scarf, how to read the sky for rain and coax feral animals near, how to purr throaty love songs in Portuguese and Basque, how to lay a vampire to rest, how to light a cigar, how to light a man's imagination on fire.

If she lived to womanhood.

If she remembered her grandmother's stories and believed them, and if none of the host of other things befell her that are always out there on the fringes of worry, like drunk drivers or lightning or zombies or a million other things. But Kizzy was ripe for goblins, and if anything got her, it would probably be them. Already one had tracked the perfume of her longing past the surly billy goat to peer in her bedroom window. Already it was studying her every move and perfecting its disguise.

· T W O ·

Butterfly Rape

On Monday, there was a new boy at Kizzy's school.

'Yum,' said Evie weakly.

'Be praised, O lords of boy flesh. We thank thee for thy bounty,' whispered Cactus.

'Amen,' said Kizzy, staring.

They weren't the only ones staring. Even Sarah Ferris craned her neck over Mick Crespain's shoulder to get a better look as Saint Pock Mark guided the new boy down the hallway.

He was tall and graceful, with a frame of broad shoulders lightly fleshed with muscle. Wheat-colored hair curled down over his collar, uncombed and lustrous. His lips were red as angels' lips in Renaissance paintings, and full and soft like angels' lips too. His eyes, very dark, canted elvishly upward at the outer corners and were surrounded by delicate bruises of sleeplessness, bluish and tender, giving him the look – Kizzy fancied – of a poet who had been up all night with a candle and a quill, memorializing a beautiful lady who had fallen from the aristocracy to die penniless of a fever, perhaps in a snowbank, leaving, of course, an ethereal corpse.

'Hell's he wearing?' Cactus asked, breaking into Kizzy's romantic reverie. 'He raid his grandfather's closet?'

'That or he stripped a dead hobo,' said Evie.

'Nah.' Cactus shook her head decisively. 'It's old-man. Look at those suspenders. Total old-man fashion.'

'Old men have fashion? Do they have, like, a catwalk?' mused Evie.

'Yeah, and he totally just stepped off it.'

'Please,' Kizzy said, glancing at the boy's strange tweedy trousers, loose at the waist, too short, and upheld by suspenders. 'That boy could wear a banana leaf and a propeller beanie and look beautiful.'

'That how you like your boys, Kiz?' asked Cactus.

'Oh yes. *All* my boys. I'll issue him a banana leaf and a propeller beanie at once and induct him into my boy-harem.'

Evie snorted. 'Boy-harem! Imagine – their little propellers all spinning around as they fan you with palm fronds.'

'While they satisfy my every whim,' added Cactus.

Kizzy snorted. 'Forget it. I don't lend out my boys.'

'Come on, no one likes a greedy slave owner.'

'My boys aren't slaves! They stay because they *want* to. I give them all the elk meat they can eat. And Xbox, you know, to keep their thumbs nice and agile.'

'Spaz,' said Evie, laughing. They leaned against the lockers and watched the new boy out of sight. Just as he rounded the far corner with Saint Pock Mark, he glanced back over his shoulder. A thrill went through Kizzy. She imagined for a second that his eyes had silvered like a cat's. And she imagined he had looked right at her. She blushed instantly, even though she was sure she was wrong. Boys' eyes didn't find her in a crowd. Boys' eyes didn't even find her when there was no one else around. They sort of glazed over or fixed on some fascinating object in the distance.

'Wonder what his name is,' she murmured after he was gone.

'Beautiful Boy, capital B, capital B,' said Cactus with a sigh. 'But, you know, *Mr.* Boy to the likes of us.'

'Yeah,' said Kizzy wistfully. 'Welcome to Saint Pock Mark's Finishing School for Cannibals, Mr. Boy.'

She went to her class wondering how long it would be before some leggy girl was sitting on his lap, snapping his old-man suspenders and tossing her silky hair. Probably by lunchtime. Jenny Glass was temporarily between boys; she'd be the lucky one. It was the natural order, Kizzy thought with a flash of bitterness at the life and hips and hair and ankles she had been dealt. Like attracts like, beauty finds beauty, and freaks look on from the smoking section, aching.

But lunchtime brought an upset to the natural order.

Kizzy met Cactus and Evie in the usual place, behind a low wall at a corner of the quad where some sort of steam billowed from a vent to disguise their cigarette smoke. They slouched there and drank Cokes and ate flat sandwiches they'd brought from home, and they could see through the cafeteria window to the corner tables. Mick Crespain's lap was vacant, and usually Kizzy's imagination would have slid her phantom right into place there, breasts resting on knuckles and all, but not today. Mr. Boy had stolen her phantom out of Mick Crespain's lap. She wondered if he had stolen Sarah Ferris out of Mick Crespain's lap too. She furtively lit a cigarette and looked around, wondering where he was.

He was much closer than she had expected. He was standing on the other side of the low wall, looking at her. Their eyes met and Kizzy instantly blushed to beet. His gaze was like physical touch, like a grabbed hand, interlaced fingers, a squeeze. Like it went through her eyes and entered her bloodstream. Her face felt molten hot.

'Hello,' he said.

'*Hello*, Mr. Boy,' she heard Cactus, behind her, say with a chuckle.

He didn't look away from Kizzy, who began to feel acutely uncomfortable. He was just *looking* at her. She felt entirely purple with blushing. 'Hi,' she murmured.

'Those things'll kill you,' he said, shifting his eyes to her cigarette. His voice was low and a little raspy.

'Yeah, well . . . maybe,' Kizzy said, looking at it too. Her heart beat fast against her ribs as she fumbled up something to say. 'But at least I'll die looking older than my age, wrinkly and dry with a gross phlegmy cough.'

He laughed. 'When you put it like that, I'm surprised anyone *doesn't* smoke.'

She was relieved to have said something, anything, instead of just staring at him and stammering. Making him laugh was a bonus, which made her blush deepen. 'Me too,' she said. 'Plus, people are always, like, *buy American*. And what's more American than cigarettes?'

He cocked his head to one side and raised an eyebrow. When his hair shifted, Kizzy saw the glint of small gold hoops in both his ears. 'You know,' she explained, babbling, 'tobacco plantations? Delightful American traditions like slavery?'

'Uh huh,' he said uncertainly.

'Nothing to do with me, though. Only slaves my people ever kept were their own children.'

He gave her a bemused look and held out his hand. 'May I?'

'What? This?' With a quizzical look, Kizzy handed him her cigarette and watched as he raised it to his red, red lips and took a long suck. Her insides shivered a little, watching his lips close over her own lipstick prints. It was the closest she had ever come to a kiss. It was a kiss by proxy. She reached for the cigarette as he handed it back. 'Do . . . do you want one?' she asked.

'No thanks. I'll just share yours.'

Kizzy could hear Evie and Cactus stifling giggles. She glanced back at them and saw their eyes were merry and astonished. She turned back to the beautiful boy, more beautiful than she had even first realized when he walked past. His face, his bones, were perfect as a statue's, like he was some Greek god's loving, handmade paean to mortal beauty. Mr. Boy was *art*. Plus, those tilted eyes gave him a sly, vulpine look that Kizzy liked. *A lot*.

Her hand trembling a little, she lifted the cigarette back to her lips and tried to seem nonchalant, but her eyes went back to his red lips as her own closed over the moistness of the filter. Exhaling, she handed him back the cigarette and pressed her lips together. Then she thought she probably looked like she was trying to kiss herself, so she hastily unpressed them.

'I'm Jack Husk, by the way,' he said, holding out his hand.

'Kizzy,' she said, reaching for it. His hand closed over hers and he squeezed gently, then trailed away, his fingertips light on her skin. Then, right then, Kizzy decided this had to be some beautiful boys' evil club initiation: to tease a freak girl and kill her heart. It was the only explanation. She hardened herself as well as she could toward Jack Husk's startling beauty and said, 'So, like, who *are* you?'

He shrugged. 'Husk comma Jack. Age seventeen. Nonsmoker.'

'Yeah, right.'

'No, really. You just corrupted virgin lungs.'

Words like 'virgin' had a way of hanging in the air, but Kizzy did her best to ignore it. 'Seriously, who are you? I mean, did you just move here or something?'

'My uncle died. I came to take care of his Christmas tree farm until after the holidays.'

'Oh. Out on the Isherwood road?'

'Yeah.'

'I live right by it. I didn't know the old guy died. Sorry. He must've been, what, like, eighty or something?'

'Actually, he was only thirty-five, but he'd smoked since he was sixteen.'

Kizzy gave him a wry smile. 'Right.'

Jack Husk smiled too. He passed back the cigarette and said, 'Really. You should quit. Cigarettes make people taste . . . *yellow*.'

Taste? Kizzy's mind did a cartwheel. *Taste?* Was this Jack Husk thinking about *tasting* her? Great God Almighty, she did not want to taste yellow if that happened, whatever yellow tasted like. She bit her lip. She didn't want to seem to be doing his bidding either, especially since this was all certainly some cruel prank, like in *Carrie*, sure to conclude with pig blood at prom. Defiantly she took a last drag of her cig and dropped it, crushing it under her heel. 'So how do nonsmokers taste?' she asked, trying to appear unruffled.

'Like licorice,' said Jack Husk promptly, the left half of his red lips pulling into an asymmetrical grin.

Kizzy could think of nothing to say but, 'Huh. I like licorice.'

'I guess you should taste a nonsmoker, then,' he said, looking into her eyes in that way that made Kizzy feel he was slipping in through them to her blood and heating up her veins from the insides.

Luckily the bell rang then and she didn't have to think of a reply. She just said, 'See you around, Jack Husk.'

'You will,' he said, cocking his head to one side and looking at her a moment longer before walking away.

Kizzy turned around to find Cactus and Evie staring at her, round-eyed. 'Did that just happen?' she demanded of them.

'Thanks a lot for introducing us!' pouted Evie.

'Jesus. Sorry. I was just trying really hard not to faint or start crying. Jesus. Seriously, that *did* just happen? It wasn't, like, a really realistic daydream?'

'Oh, it happened,' said Cactus. 'Kizzy! You just mingled saliva with the most beautiful boy ever to tread the hallways of Saint Pock's. *Saliva*. There's *DNA* in saliva. You're, like, carrying his *cells* in your mouth like one of those weird frogs that incubates its eggs in its cheeks!'

With a squeal, Evie added, 'You could have his *mouth baby!*'

'God! Only you guys could make his saliva sound gross. I mean, did you *see* how perfect?'

'Oh, I saw,' said Cactus.

'He was totally *staring* at you, Kiz,' marveled Evie.

'Hell would he want to do that?' she muttered.

The girls climbed back over the low wall and headed inside with the student herd, and Kizzy floated through the rest of her classes in a daze.

She saw Jack Husk after school, leaning against the flagpole in his long-limbed, easy way. She wondered if he was waiting for her, and then felt ridiculous for wondering. Of course he wasn't. But he was. He straightened up when she came out, and tilted his head to motion her near. 'Hey, Kizzy,' he said softly.

'Hey, Jack Husk.'

'Listen, I was wondering,' he started, but paused, seeming a little sheepish. 'I have this clothing situation.' He motioned to his old-man pants.

'Yeah? Don't worry about it. Probably half the sheep here are going to show up tomorrow in their grandparents' stuff.'

He laughed. 'Well, I need to get some clothes anyway. I thought maybe you could show me where to go.'

'Oh, sure,' Kizzy said, a little disappointed. For a second she thought he'd waited to walk home with her, since they were going the same way. 'There's this second-hand store I go to, it's pretty cool and cheap. It's up by the gas station and the pizza place with the solar system hanging from the ceiling.' She started to point the way, but Jack Husk caught her hand in the air and held her fist inside his own for a moment like it was some small delicate thing, like a tulip bulb or an egg.

He said, 'No, I meant, I thought you could *show* me, and . . . *help* me.'

'Oh,' said Kizzy faintly.

'Unless you have somewhere to be.'

'No, I just have to be home in time to make dinner. But I can go with you for a little while.'

'Great.' He smiled. Not the skewed half-smile, but a full and lovely one that dazzled her.

They started walking, and Kizzy turned around to wave to Cactus and Evie, who flashed her quick maniac grins behind

Jack Husk's back. As they passed through a crowd that included Jenny Glass, Kizzy heard someone whisper, 'What's the new guy doing with Butterfly Rape?' and her heart instantly cinched into a tight knot.

She hoped Jack Husk hadn't heard, but as soon as they were clear of the crowd, he looked at her with one eyebrow cocked and asked, 'What did that girl just call you?'

Kizzy grimaced. 'Forget it.'

'Okay.' He paused, then looked at her again. 'Because it sounded like *butterfly rape*.'

Mortified, Kizzy nodded. 'Yep,' she said, popping the *p* sound. 'That's me.'

He looked puzzled. 'Why?'

Turning purple once more, Kizzy chewed her lip and finally said, 'Well, freshman year, before I learned *not* to participate in class discussions, we were talking about human nature or something in Life Science, and this girl Heather Black starts saying how humans are the only violent species, and how noble the animal kingdom is, blah-de-blah-blah, only killing for food, and the only species that has, like, war and murder and rape, is humans.'

Jack Husk snorted. 'I guess she hasn't met any orangutans.'

'What?'

'Orangutans rape. They even gang rape.'

'Oh. Well, I'm glad I didn't know that then. My nickname could be worse.'

'What, you told this girl that *butterflies* rape?'

'Yeah. Well, they *do*. Some kinds, anyway. The males will, like, wait for a female to hatch out of her chrysalis and rape her before she can even fly. Like, welcome to the world, lovely butterfly. Then, as if that's not bad enough, they secrete this stuff into her that hardens like a plug, so she can't mate with any other males – though, after her first, you know, *date*, I don't know why she'd want to. Then the males adapted these things on their feet for gouging out the plug, so they adapted again, and started secreting, like, a whole shell over her abdomen, like a chastity belt that can't be gouged off. Isn't that insane?'

'Did you make that up?' Jack Husk asked, looking a little repulsed.

'Could anyone make that up? There's crazy shit in nature, like these spores that invade a caterpillar's body and turn it into a *vegetable*, and then cannibals use it to make tattoo ink. How sci-fi is that? I told Heather Black she watched too many cartoons. Animals do too murder. Chimpanzees even kill each other's babies sometimes. Humans are not the only species to kill for territory, for dominance—'

'For fun,' added Jack Husk.

'Ooh.' Kizzy wrinkled her nose at him. 'Serial killer comment.'

'Not *me*,' he said, elbowing her playfully. 'I meant *cats*.'

'Yeah. Weirdo. Anyway, that's where I got my charming nickname.'

'Sucks.'

'Yeah. I shouldn't even have argued. Heather Black might be a stupid cow, but I basically agree with her. Humans are totally the worst. We're vile.'

'Yeah, you can be,' Jack Husk agreed. 'The thing is, you throw brains and souls into an animal and stir, you don't really know what you're going to get. If humans are going to be vile, they're going to be a bigger and better kind of vile than, like, a *dog* could ever be.'

'When they were good, they were *very very good*, and when they were bad, they were *horrid*,' said Kizzy.

He laughed. 'Yeah, totally. I like that. Which are you, Kizzy? Very very good, or horrid?' He cocked his head and squinted at her like he was trying to decide.

'Oh, horrid,' she replied at once.

'Yeah,' he said, his eyes seeming to flash silver again. 'Me too.'

They reached the thrift store and he opened the door for her.

This was where Kizzy always shopped instead of the mall, partly because her parents barely gave her any money, and partly because it had a trifold changing screen of embossed, moth-eaten velvet that looked like a remnant from Marie Antoinette's boudoir. She loved to sling an armful of cheap dresses over it and try them on one by one, with mismatched gossamer scarves, platform boots, and cat glasses. Sometimes she even bought that stuff, though she only ever wore jeans where anyone would see her.

She steered Jack Husk away from jeans, though, and dressed him like the sleepy poet she'd first imagined him to be, in a black velvet jacket with threadbare elbows, a white shirt with a little bit of red embroidery to look like a drop of blood, and pinstriped pants the proper length for his long legs. They picked up a broken pocket watch from a mosaic bowl full of junk jewelry, and Kizzy had him put on some old leather aviator goggles for fun, and he liked them and bought them too.

'This stuff's even weirder than what I was already wearing,' he said, looking at himself in the mirror. 'I look like I live in an attic.'

'That is *exactly* the look I was going for,' Kizzy said, pleased.

'What about you?' he asked. He held up an emerald silk scarf with fringe.

'Nah.' She waved it away.

'Nah? You've got me in goggles. You can at least try on a scarf. Here.' He threaded it under her hair and tied it into a floppy bow on top of her head. Her whole scalp tingled from the gentle probing of his fingers in the thicket of her hair.

She looked in the mirror. 'I look like a drunk cleaning lady,' she said flatly.

'Try it like a gypsy.'

She did, and kind of liked it.

'I'm going to buy it for you,' said Jack Husk.

'No,' Kizzy protested. 'It's way overpriced. And I won't wear it.'

'Why not?'

'You don't understand. There are girls at school whose only purpose in life is to make up nasty nicknames when anyone does something the slightest bit out of the ordinary.'

'Come on, Kizzy. It'd have to be a step up from Butterfly Rape.'

Kizzy laughed and it came out as a throaty chuckle, almost a purr, the closest she had yet come to the sultry voice she would grow into as she grew up and learned how to wear her skin. *If* she grew up. She relented on the green scarf. 'Okay, then. Thank you.'

Jack Husk paid the woman behind the counter, who'd been unable to take her eyes off him since they entered. Turning back to Kizzy, he pulled out his new broken pocket watch and pretended to consult it. 'Time to prepare the feast?' he asked.

'Feast!' she scoffed. 'Try elk burgers. With my secret ingredient, of course.'

'Oh yeah? What's that?'

'Well, the secret ingredient is supposed to be love. But I substitute scorn. Just a pinch. A little goes a long way.'

'Sounds delicious,' he said. 'Come on. I'll walk with you.'

'Okay.'

It was much easier than Kizzy would have thought, walking across town with a beautiful boy, talking about things like the fat content of elk meat and the aerodynamic quality of pizza, and about the jocks of Saint Pock's, and superstition, and marshmallows, and death.

'My grandmother died last summer,' Kizzy told him, surprised as the words tumbled out of her mouth.

'Yeah? Sorry to hear it. She buried in there?' He hooked a thumb at the cemetery as they passed it.

'Nah. We plant our bones in our own soil.'

'Really? Why?'

Kizzy shrugged. 'My family's weird.' She wasn't about to tell Jack Husk about the swans' wings and the singing, and the ghosts slipping from their graves to begin their next adventure. 'Your uncle buried there?' she asked.

'Uh-uh. Cremated.'

'Oh.' Kizzy shivered. 'God.' Her people believed cremation trapped the soul in the body and then shattered it into millions of tiny flakes of ash. 'Did you know him well?'

'Hardly at all.' Jack Husk was still wearing his aviator goggles and they disguised some of his beauty, but not the most distracting part: his red lips. Kizzy could barely look at them without thinking of kissing. Of being tasted.

Too quickly, they arrived at the Christmas tree farm. Neat rows of trees stretched back toward the misty hills where Kizzy's uncles hunted. 'Home sweet home,' said Jack Husk, motioning to the little trailer.

Kizzy eyed it. She'd never thought much about it when the old man lived here. He was always outside working, planting trees or digging them up or cutting them down. He'd hitched at his suspenders and waved sometimes when she walked by, and she'd waved back, probably without much enthusiasm, and she'd never imagined him inside the trailer, living in it. But she couldn't help imagining Jack Husk sleeping in a dead man's narrow little bed. 'Cozy,' she said unconvincingly.

'As a coffin,' he replied.

The fat dog lifted his head up slowly and looked at them. 'You inherit him too?' Kizzy asked.

'I guess so.'

'Laziest dog I've ever seen,' she said. But then the lazy dog, the dog that Kizzy walked past every single day and who couldn't even be bothered to bark, curled his snout into a snarl.

'He's not crazy about me,' Jack Husk said as the snarl grew louder.

'I guess not.'

The fat old dog actually rose to his feet, something Kizzy had rarely witnessed, and with his head lowered and his teeth bared in a vicious growl, he looked much more menacing than she'd have thought possible. Jack Husk frowned and pushed back his goggles onto his forehead, making his hair stick out in tufts. Anyone else might have looked silly, but he looked like he was posing for one of those fashion spreads in *Rolling Stone* magazine where bored, beautiful people loll around like they're waiting for the bus in Purgatory, usually with some nipple showing. 'Well,' he said, 'I'd better deal with him.'

'What are you going to do?'

'Honestly? Give him a wide berth and slip around the back. But I'll wait until you're gone so you can't see me scramble if he comes after me.'

Kizzy laughed. 'Maybe I'd better watch, you know, just in case.'

Smiling the crooked smile, he said, 'No. Go. Please. It's unspeakably uncool to be seen dodging fat dogs.'

'Okay, then. See you around, Jack Husk. Be careful.'

'See you in the morning, Kizzy,' he said, and Kizzy felt, for an instant, as if her blood fizzed inside her like champagne.

· **THREE** ·

Ripe as a Plum

After dinner had been cooked and eaten – scorn and all – Kizzy went to her room and closed the door. She sat on the end of her bed and looked at herself in the mirror. Really *looked*. She was still wearing the green scarf, and though her hair billowed out at the nape of her neck, wild and coarse as always, it was captured flat around her face and hidden, not springing up in its usual topiary way. The effect was to bring her face into focus, and Kizzy stared at it for minutes, getting the feeling that something had happened to her since the last time she had looked at herself, if indeed she ever really had.

She saw proud cheekbones beginning to rise out of the thick husk of adolescence. She saw a coy curl in the corners of her lips, lips that had *practically* touched Jack Husk's lips. Staring at her face, she began to fancy her outer layer had begun to melt away while she wasn't paying attention, and something – some new skeleton – was emerging from beneath the softness of her accustomed self. With a deep, visceral ache, she wished her true form might prove to be a sleek and shining one, like a stiletto blade slicing free of an ungainly sheath. Like a bird of prey losing its hatchling fluff to hunt in cold, magnificent skies. That she might become something glittering, something startling, something dangerous.

Kizzy wanted to be a woman who would dive off the prow of a sailboat into the sea, who would fall back in a tangle of sheets, laughing, and who could dance a tango, lazily stroke a leopard with her bare foot, freeze an enemy's blood with her eyes, make promises she couldn't possibly keep, and then shift the world to keep them. She wanted to write memoirs and autograph them at a tiny bookshop in Rome, with a line of admirers snaking down a pink-lit alley. She wanted to make love on a balcony, ruin someone, trade in esoteric knowledge, watch strangers as coolly as a cat. She wanted to be inscrutable, have a drink named after her, a love song written for her, and a handsome adventurer's small airplane, champagne-christened *Kizzy*, which would vanish one day in a windstorm in Arabia so that she would have to mount a rescue operation involving camels, and wear an indigo veil against the stinging sand, just like the nomads.

Kizzy *wanted*.

She pushed back her shoulders from her usual sullen slouch and made an effort to sit up straight. It felt unnatural; her sinews resisted. She had a sudden terrifying thought that if she had waited, if she had gone on as she was, her poor posture might have calcified like that. She might have hardened into a slumped carapace of a person who would never, *could never*, throw back her shoulders, walk tall, taunt vampires with her white throat, toss her head in joy or disdain. She would have curled over herself like a toenail left too long untrimmed. She flushed now, looking at her reflection, shoulders low and calm, neck elongated, almost elegant, light moving over her green silk scarf like a river, and she felt a sense of narrow escape in the ache of this new posture. As if she could still become someone else.

Maybe Jack Husk had already glimpsed that new girl within her, guessed how she was ready to slice free in one clean move like a stiletto blade flicking forth. She thought of his perfect face and sly eyes, his hand catching hers in the air, of his lingering gaze, and the sensation of being penetrated by it. And looking at herself in the mirror, minute after minute, unveiling herself to herself, she began at last to see her great-aunt Mairenni looking out at her, filled with her hungers and her secrets, and radiant with her weird, succulent beauty.

Ripe as a plum ready to drop from its branch at the lightest touch.

Kizzy slept restlessly and dreamed many things that night – lips and fingers and fruit, and Jack Husk taking off his goggles and tasting her, beginning with the tender insides of her wrists. Strange images came to her all night, and she was greeted by another strange sight when she was awakened in the morning by the wretched cry of the peacock right outside her window.

She opened her eyes. A swan feather drifted past her face, twirled when her breath caught it, and sailed to the floor. She blinked, sat up, blinked again. The room was asift with swan feathers. They were settling to the floor as if she had just missed the strange storm that had deposited them here. A glint on her pillow drew her eye and she turned to see, laid alongside the impression of her head, the mother-of-pearl handle she knew so well, and tucked up quietly within it, resting now, her grandmother's stiletto, back from the grave.

She reached for it, and it was cold as a mountain winter in her hand.

The first thing Kizzy did was check the small circle of family graves in the back field. She stood there in her nightgown, the knife clutched in her fist, looking at the undisturbed ground of her grandmother's grave. She felt the stir of ghosts all around. She *would* feel them now. It was fall, after the harvest and before the first freeze – this was the time when the veil between the worlds was draggled and thin, and voices murmured through its sodden membrane from the other side. It was always in the fall that Kizzy felt the ghosts lingering about, skittish as stray cats and drawn by the same thing: the whiff of food.

The cats came for the odor of the smokehouse where Kizzy's father and uncles made sausages from the various things they killed. With their little rough tongues, the cats lapped up pooling blood before it could congeal in the dirt. The ghosts had no such thirst, but came for the clumps of asphodel that bloomed round the graves all summer, and for the bowls of boiled barley the rest of the year. Cats and ghosts both partook of the saucers of milk and that was okay. They consumed different parts of it: the cats its substance, the ghosts its essence, and none went to waste.

They came from afar, cats and ghosts both, because normal families didn't spill hot blood in their driveways or leave out food for the dead, and they weren't exactly spoiled for choice. Kizzy thought most of the ghostly visitors came from the cemetery down the road; surely all the spirits in her family's little plot had moved along, well provisioned as they were with coin, food, weapon, and wing for their journey. Surely *they* didn't linger here. Surely her grandmother hadn't.

How, then, had her knife come to be on Kizzy's pillow, and her swan's wing, torn feather from feather, in Kizzy's room? Kizzy frowned, puzzled, and went back in the house, passing her mother in the kitchen and choosing not to speak of the feathers and knife. Her people would be terribly disturbed by it; they'd surely keep Kizzy home from school to scry the meaning of the ominous visitation, to bless the grave, and to try to return the knife to its rightful owner. And Kizzy did worry that her grandmother's ghost was weaponless and vulnerable in the shadowed land. But her mind kept turning back to Jack Husk. She had to see him again, to see if he was *real*, so she said nothing of the knife.

She showered, dried her hair, and tied, untied, and retied the green scarf, deciding at last to go ahead and wear it. She pulled on a pair of jeans and a sweater and slid her grandmother's stiletto into her back pocket. She had a cup of coffee and a cigarette, brushed her teeth three times to scour away any yellow flavor, put on lipstick and then wiped it off, hopeful of kissing and scowling at her own absurd hope, and she almost left the house. But at the last minute she pulled off her clothes and stepped into a vintage dress she'd bought at the thrift store and never worn. It was made of apple-green kimono silk in a rippling pattern, with a mandarin collar and a row of big black buttons all the way down the front. She stood in front of the mirror for a minute, watching the way the silk slipped and shone when she moved her hips, then she pulled on black boots and hurried out the door.

Jack Husk was waiting for her in front of the Christmas tree farm, and he whistled low when he saw her. 'Great dress,' he said, his eyes sliding all the way down the row of buttons.

'Thanks,' Kizzy said, blushing just as deeply as she had the day before, at school. She'd have to get used to him all over again, taking small sips of his beauty as if it was too hot a drink to swallow all at once. One shy glance revealed to her that Jack Husk wasn't carrying his new school books but a picnic basket. 'What's that?' she asked.

He held it up and smiled, mischievous as an imp. 'Breakfast picnic,' he said. There was a checked blanket folded carelessly under the basket's handles. 'Care to join me?'

'What, *now*? What about school?'

Jack Husk shrugged. 'I'm not such a huge fan.'

'Yeah, me either.'

'Good. Then you'll come with me.' He held out his arm for her in an old-fashioned, courtly gesture, and there was no question in Kizzy's mind how she would be spending her morning. She hooked her arm through Jack Husk's, laying her fingers lightly on the velvet nap of his sleeve, and walked beside him, noticing as she turned that the old man's dog was not in his place on the porch.

'Everything go okay with the dog yesterday?' she asked.

'Sure,' he answered. 'No problem. So, is there a park around here somewhere?'

Kizzy shook her head. 'Just the cemetery.'

'Oh, well, that'll work. Yeah?'

It was just ahead, behind a neat fence. Kizzy walked past it every day, but she hadn't been in it for years, not since she was a child and snuck there to listen to the snatches of ghost conversation that blew in on an icy wind from the next world. It wasn't a Gothic cemetery; there were no mossy angels weeping miraculous tears of blood, no crypts or curses or crumble. No poets or courtesans were buried here; no vampires slumbered belowground. It was only a collection of stone rectangles standing straight and ordinary. Even the dead loitering here spoke of dull things, like the one who worried she'd left the stove burning when she died.

But it didn't have to be some fabulous Parisian cemetery for the idea of a picnic in it to bloom in Kizzy's imagination into something daring. She imagined herself telling Evie and Cactus. A *breakfast picnic* in the *cemetery* with *Jack Husk*! Their eyes would bulge with glee and envy and they'd want to know everything. They'd want to know if he'd kissed her. She stole a glance at him and caught him looking at her lips, and she looked away, blushing hotly, and found the voice to say, 'Yeah, okay,' in what she hoped was a casual way.

They went through the cemetery gate, arm in arm in their antique clothing, and it was then that the ghosts, all of a sudden and with only a flitter of grass blades for a warning, hit Kizzy like a maelstrom.

Her skirt flared and twisted itself tight to her legs as a rush of cold wind swept around her. It circled deasil, thrice, just like her grandmother's ghost had done the day of her burial. But Kizzy felt a whole swelling of ghosts around her this time, a tide; her grandmother might have been there, but she wasn't alone. Kizzy froze in mid-step, chilled and startled, and looked up at Jack Husk. For a second some look passed through his sly eyes, some intelligence . . . a hint of a sneer? And Kizzy almost thought he knew the sudden wind for what it was: an onslaught of ghosts. Had they swept around her only, she wondered now, or around them both? Had they included Jack Husk in their circle of protection? Or had they wound up Kizzy alone? Had that wind tried to slide between them, like a wall?

'Brrr . . .' he said, shivering slightly. To Kizzy's dismay, he unhooked his arm from hers, but then he settled it around her shoulder, drawing her neatly against his side, and her dismay evaporated, along with any question she'd had about his awareness of rampant ghosts. 'Cold wind,' he said simply.

'Mm hm,' Kizzy agreed. The velvet of his jacket was now snug against her cheek, and there was very little room to think of anything else but the feel of it, and of the way she'd caught him looking at her lips, and what that might mean.

As they walked through the cemetery, tucked together, she heard words as she used to when she came here as a child, snippets of speech as murky as gutter water draining through a clog of leaves. 'The wintermen are gleaning,' said one, and another intoned 'butterfly,' and 'hungry.' 'Stove burning,' said a flat voice, and then suddenly, a familiar voice hissed, '—*knife, Sunshine*—'

Kizzy's eyes went wide and she looked around and over her shoulder, inadvertently nuzzling Jack Husk's hand with her chin. Despite that smooth jolt of a touch, she had the wherewithal to realize she'd left her grandmother's knife in her jeans pocket. All the years of wanting it and she'd left it behind! She wanted to ask her grandmother what she was doing here. She should be far away by now, navigating labyrinths, fending off shadows, lapping water from stalactite tips with her ghostly tongue, and answering riddles to win passage through gates made of bones. She should be singing beasts to sleep with lullabies and bribing otherworldly coyotes to smuggle her deeper into her new world. She shouldn't be *here*, among these fainthearted cemetery ghosts! This eternal loitering wasn't for Kizzy's folk, least of all her grandmother, her strong, untemptable grandmother. Kizzy wanted to ask her – but she was warm against Jack Husk's side and didn't want to step away from him to whisper her question to the dead.

'Did you hear something?' Jack Husk asked suddenly.

'What?' Kizzy asked, startled and strangely guilty, as if he'd caught her hoarding the whispers of the ghosts to herself.

'I don't know. Sounded like a twig snapping. I wonder if anyone else is here.'

But there didn't seem to be anyone else in the cemetery, or even any sign of recent visitors. It was a lonesome place, and Kizzy wasn't surprised the ghosts came to her messy yard to while away their days among the cats and chickens.

Jack Husk's fingers began idly stroking Kizzy's shoulder as they walked between the rows of graves. It happened slowly, imperceptibly, but she realized he was pulling her little by little closer to him, the stroking deepening into rubbing, so his whole hand was cupped over her shoulder, his thumb making little circles. She could smell boy spice beneath the thrift-store aroma of his jacket, and the rubbing and the smell began to work to soften her – like butter before you add sugar, in the first step of making something sweet. It was her first experience of how bodies could meld together, how breath could slip naturally into rhythm. It was hypnotic. Heady.

And she wanted more.

'They have teeth,' whispered a ghost. Kizzy ignored it.

'They have nectar,' said another, very faint and filled with longing. Kizzy felt a small chill, but ignored that too.

'Hungry?' Jack Husk asked, as they pivoted to walk another cemetery row.

Kizzy shrugged. She had little interest in eating just now. But spreading out the checked blanket someplace quiet and sitting down, leaning back on her elbows beside Jack Husk, that *did* interest her. She couldn't stop glancing at his lips, and she kept pressing her own together, hyperaware of them. She remembered babysitting an infant cousin on the day he'd discovered his tongue; he'd kept wagging it and touching it, making a whole repertoire of new sounds and trying to stick it out far enough to see it, obsessed by the discovery of this new appendage. Kizzy felt like that about her lips today, like she was just now finding out what they were for, but she hoped she was more discreet than her baby cousin had been.

'Let's go over there,' Jack Husk said, nodding his head toward a distant corner of the cemetery where there looked to be a sort of overgrown garden. They made their way slowly, Kizzy scarcely noticing the graves they passed, so wrapped up was she in this newness of strolling like lovers, slow and fused. But at the end of the row of graves, she did notice something.

She walked on past it; it took a moment to register, but a few steps later her head swung around and she looked again, recognition tingling in her.

The frowsy green of the unkempt cemetery lawn was disturbed by a patch of brown, stark as a wound. It seemed to describe a radius around one particular grave, and Kizzy squinted to see what the tombstone said. She couldn't read it, and Jack Husk was tugging her gently in the other direction. She surprised herself by reaching for his velvet lapel and tugging him back. 'Over here,' she said. 'I want to see something.'

'What?' he asked, coming easily along with her.

'This.' She stopped before it. A grave where nothing grew, not even grass. She read the name on the headstone. *Amy Ingersoll*. 'I knew her,' Kizzy said, surprised.

'You did?' asked Jack Husk.

Kizzy nodded. 'I was a freshman. I think she was a junior, but I barely saw her because she got taken out of school. She was sick. She . . .' Kizzy's voice trailed off. She had almost said, *She starved herself to death.* But seeing this dead brown grave, other words came to her mind. *She wasted away.*

'Sad,' said Jack Husk. 'She was your age when she died.'

'Yeah,' said Kizzy, thinking of the picture of gaunt Amy Ingersoll she'd seen in the paper, her eyes seeming huge and haunted in her pinched face. There had been a special assembly in school about eating disorders. A doctor had talked about anorexia and bulimia. After, Kizzy and Evie had pinched the generous skin of their hips and joked crassly that they could use a little anorexia themselves, and Cactus had said they could start by switching to Diet Coke.

'I wonder why the grass is all dead here,' Kizzy said, wanting there to be some other explanation than the one buzzing in her thoughts. Surely in this dull town the wild things her family believed in were just stories. Such things happened far from here, on cobblestones, and in the haunted dooryards of ancient churches.

'Damned,' said a ghost right in Kizzy's ear. She shivered.

Jack Husk felt it and let go of her shoulder to shrug off his velvet jacket. 'You're cold,' he said. 'Here.' He draped it over her shoulders and drew her back against him. Her brow rested against his jaw briefly, skin against skin. 'Come on,' he urged.

She went with him to the little garden in the corner, and Jack Husk laid out his checked blanket behind some stone urns overflowing with ivy and scant alyssum blossoms left over from summer. They settled down and he opened his picnic basket and produced from it a loaf of golden bread and a round cheese with an artisan's stamp in its thick rind. Things like that, cheeses signed like artworks, were unknown in Kizzy's house, where they had either salty lumpish cheese her mother made or an army-feeding slab of impossibly orange stuff from the superstore.

Tucking her dress around her knees, Kizzy watched Jack Husk lay out purple linen napkins and a real silver knife with just a hint of tarnish on it, and then a footed silver bowl of chocolates wrapped in foil, and she was wide-eyed with the elegance of it. If she had ever thought to dream up a cemetery picnic, the cemetery would have been a different, better one – in Paris or New Orleans, somewhere with moss and broken statues – but the picnic would have been just like this.

'Nice,' she murmured inadequately. Jack Husk smiled at her, and he was so beautiful it almost hurt. A wave of skepticism swept over her, not for the first time. *Why*, she wondered. *Why me?*

'Silly girl—' she heard or imagined her grandmother hissing in her ear.

'Chocolate first,' said Jack Husk, the raspy edge of his voice erasing the faint, ghostly one. 'That's my only picnic rule.'

'Well, *okay*,' Kizzy said, feigning reluctance and unwrapping one of the chocolates. It was so dark it was almost black and it melted on her tongue into an ancient flavor of seed pod, earth, shade, and sunlight, its bitterness casting just a shadow of sweet. It tasted . . . *fine*, so subtle and strange it made her feel like a novitiate into some arcanum of spice.

The cheese was the same, so different from anything she'd tasted she could scarcely tell if it was wonderful or terrible. They nibbled it with the bread, and Jack Husk asked Kizzy if she thought it was too early in the day for wine, which he produced from his basket and poured into dainty etched glasses no bigger than Dixie cups.

It was as earthy and dark as the chocolate and Kizzy sipped it slowly, softening and softening, stretched out on one elbow, her hip full as an odalisque's hip, a lush hummock of apple green for Jack Husk to lay his head on, and he did, and closed his eyes while Kizzy lightly teased the ends of his unruly hair.

After a little while he sat up and reached one more time into his basket. He took out an apricot, which he cupped in his hand, and a peach, which he handed to Kizzy. She took it and held it. Its skin was as soft as the velvet of Jack Husk's jacket and the scent . . . she could smell the honey sweetness of it even through the skin, and she lifted it and took a deeper breath. *Nectar*, she thought dreamily. But she didn't take a bite. She didn't want the juices dribbling down her chin. She just smelled it again and watched Jack Husk eat his apricot and toss the pit. Then he leaned back against one of the stone urns, arranging the billow of ivy and blossoms around his head to look like a wig.

Kizzy laughed. 'It's a good look for you,' she said.

'Like it? Here.' He lifted a heavy cluster of ivy beside his head to make a wig for her too, and he motioned her to sit close. She scooted into the space at his side and held still as he arranged the flowers over her forehead, pausing to gently tuck one stray curl of her real hair back under her scarf.

His face was so near hers. She couldn't keep her eyes from straying to his lips; she could smell the sweetness of apricot on his breath, see a trace of moisture on his red lips. He was looking at her lips too. She was suddenly very nervous. He leaned closer. Kizzy froze, not knowing whether to close her eyes or leave them open. She had a horror of being one of those girls in movies who closes her eyes and puckers up while the boy sits back and smirks.

And seconds later she was glad she hadn't closed her eyes, because Jack Husk didn't kiss her. He took the peach from her hand, lifted it to his lips, and took a bite. So close, the perfume it released was like a drug, and Kizzy had a powerful urge to lean in and taste it too, to taste the nectar on his lips. She couldn't take her eyes off his lips. She moved forward ever so slightly. Jack Husk saw, and leaned closer.

This time it was real; it was really going to happen. Kizzy was going to kiss a beautiful boy. Why then was she thinking about the peach, of how his lips would taste of it?

Why was she imagining how delicious Jack Husk's kiss would be?

She stared at him, and at the periphery of her vision something glinted. It was the little silver knife, still impaled in the rind of the cheese. *Knife*, she thought. Her fingers twitched, wanting to reach for it, as some kind of knowing skimmed the glassy surface of her mind. All the omens of the day, the swirl of swan feathers, the grave of dead grass, her grandmother's blade still rimed with the frost of the underworld, all her memories of warnings, they coalesced into a simple understanding: deep in her veins ran the admonition never to eat fruit out of season. It was late autumn; all orchards were bare, and no peach trafficked in from a far hemisphere could smell so sweet. Surely only one orchard could have ripened it.

With that, Kizzy knew. A goblin had her soul on the end of his fishing line, ready to reel it in. She knew. But now, in the fugue of *wanting*, of *almost having*, filled with the musk and the spice of that wine and that chocolate, her hip still warm from Jack Husk's head, the knowing was as insubstantial as words written on water. Every trace of it vanished as soon as it was written, leaving only the reflection of Jack Husk's too-perfect beauty. It was an imaginary beauty dreamed up just to please her, and it did. It did. It pleased and drugged her. Her eyelids were heavy but her soul was light as gossamer, a spider's web in a wind, anchored only by a single thread.

Kizzy *knew*, but she willfully *unknew* it, and the plangent voices of the dead were lost to the drum of her hot blood and the tingle of her ready lips. She wanted to taste and be tasted.

She didn't reach for the knife. Heavily and hypnotically, with her soul flattening itself back like the ears of a hissing cat, Kizzy leaned in and drank of Jack Husk's full, moist mouth, and his red, red lips were hungry against hers, drinking her in return. Their eyes closed. Fingers clutched at collars and hair, at the picnic blanket, at the grass. And as they sank down, pinning their shadows beneath them, the horizon tipped on its side, and slowly, thickly, hour by hour, the day spilled out and ebbed away.

It was Kizzy's first kiss, and maybe it was her last, and it was delicious.

· SPICY LITTLE CURSES ·
SUCH AS THESE

Kissing can ruin lives. Lips touch, sometimes teeth clash. New hunger is born with a throb and caution falls away. A cursed girl with lips still moist from her first kiss might feel suddenly wild, like a little monsoon. She might forget her curse just long enough to get careless and let it come true. She might kill everyone she loves.

She might, and she might not.

A particular demon in India rather hoped that she would.

This is the story of the curse and the kiss, the demon and the girl. It's a love story with dancing and death in it, and singing and souls and shadows reeled out on kite strings. It begins underneath India, on the cusp of the last century when the British were still riding elephants with maharajas and skirmishing on the arid frontiers of the empire.

The story begins in Hell.

The Demon & the Old Bitch

Down in Hell, the Englishwoman known around Jaipur as 'the old bitch' was taking tea with a demon. She was silver-haired, straight-backed, and thin-lipped, with a stare that could shoot laughter from the air like game birds. She was not at all liked by her countrymen, but even they would have been shocked to see her here.

'Come to the point,' she told the demon impatiently.

If he looked faintly human, it was because once upon a time he had been. He was little and ancient, with a moon-round face as withered as old apple peel, half of it colored red like a wine stain. 'Remember, my dear,' he replied with a genial smile, 'a handful may survive naturally. Earthquakes are full of surprises. Children still alive, like buried treasure? It makes the spirit soar to see them pulled out into the sunlight.'

'Indeed,' she said.

There had been an earthquake in Kashmir. She had sent her shadow out to see it, and it had slipped among the ruins of villages, relaying the devastation back to her through its dulled senses. Shadows have no ears, so she couldn't hear the lamentations of the survivors, which was as she preferred. She said, 'You will give me the children, Vasudev. You know there's no arguing with me on this matter.'

'Estella, you wouldn't deprive me of the pleasure of our negotiations, would you? They're what I *live* for.'

'You haven't been *alive* for a thousand years. If you were, you might take less pleasure in bartering for children's souls.'

'Do you think so? I scarcely remember what it was like, being alive. I recall certain . . . *appetites*. The sight of a woman's navel could drive me mad. Children, though? I have absolutely no memory of caring anything about them.' He poured tea out into chipped cups and added sugar and cream to his own.

Estella took hers and sipped it black, replying bitterly, 'I well believe that.' It was Vasudev's particular way with children that accounted for her being here at all, a lone living human descending each day into Hell.

There was a tonic the demons brewed to keep their ancient flesh whole when they passed through the flames. More than fifty herbs and barks went into it, along with the mixed waters of sacred rivers. Once, many years ago, Vasudev had forgotten to drink his daily dose and he'd been burned passing through the Fire. Half his face had remained this vivid crimson ever since, and when he went up into the living world, children *stared* at him. And while he had never been overly disposed to spare their souls before, he began to become downright perverse about it, culling the young at every opportunity. Even when some more likely candidate might be lying by – an ailing grandparent flush with memories of a long life, for example – he would take the child instead, every time.

Yama, the Lord of Hell, had seen that some balance was called for, and he had appointed Estella to parley on behalf of the children. For more than forty years now she had served as Ambassador to Hell.

She calmly sipped her tea and said, 'Ten.'

'Ten?' Vasudev chuckled. 'How sentimental of you. What would people say? They'd call it a miracle.'

'A miracle never hurt anyone.'

He thought it over. 'Ten children clambering out of the rubble, white with the dust of their ruined village. Those great dark eyes of theirs . . . No. It's too many. It's too *rosy*. The little beasts will come to *expect* to survive. I'll give you five. Or, if you're game,' he said, his small eyes glinting, 'we can spice things up with a little curse.'

'I despise your curses,' Estella said with a shudder, then added, after a pause, 'Eight.'

'Eight?' Vasudev scoffed. 'No, I don't think so. Not today. You can have five, or you can let me have some fun.'

Estella felt a weight settle on her heart. Vasudev got in these peevish moods sometimes, and she knew he would dig in his heels now, and tomorrow, and the next day, until he had his fun, and she never knew what form his 'fun' might take. He might give her a few extra children in the bargain, but only on the condition they grow forked tails, or never fall in love, or wake screaming every night for the rest of their lives. He had endless imagination for curses.

Wearily, wearily, Estella asked, 'What do you have in mind?'

Vasudev laughed and swung his little legs in his chair. His feet didn't quite reach the ground. 'I'll tell you what I have in mind. You can have your ten Kashmiri brats . . . *for free* . . .'

'Free?' Estella repeated. No soul was ever free. Every child she saved she purchased in trade. It was her own dark work to select

those who would die in their place, and she had an ever-changing list of the wicked from whom to choose. High up on it now were a slave trader in the Aravalli Hills and a captain in Calcutta who had kicked his groom to death because his horse threw a shoe. Heart attack, drowning, a fall from a horse, they would meet such ends as that. Estella always dealt sudden deaths, even to those who most deserved lingering ones.

This was the office she had performed since she was a young widow and had found her way down to Hell on her own, like Orpheus of myth. Unlike Orpheus, though, who had charmed his way past the three-headed dog and enchanted Persephone with his lyre, Estella had had no music at her fingertips with which to win Yama's sympathy. He had *not* given her her young husband to guide back up to the world. Instead, he had given her this job to do. It was an ugly job – earthquakes, floods, pestilence, murder, souls slipping always through her fingers – and her resentful demon counterpart took every opportunity to make it uglier.

'No, really,' he insisted. '*Free!* Ten children shall survive and no one shall die in trade for it! All you have to do is deliver a curse I've been dreaming up. The Political Agent's wife, the songbird, you know the one? She's had another brat and the christening is tonight. Were you invited? No? Well, that oughtn't stop you. Here is what I want you to do . . .'

He told her his idea.

Estella blanched. 'No!' she said at once, appalled.

'No? *No?* All right then, how about this? I'll give you *all* of them. Every child in that village!'

'Every . . . ?'

'Every last brat will live! How can you say no to that?'

73

She couldn't say no, as well he knew. She would have nightmares over this curse for the rest of her life, and Vasudev knew that too, and that was his favorite thing about it. After a long, miserable silence, Estella nodded.

Vasudev chuckled and chortled and went off whistling, leaving Estella to her work. Still pale, she took a flask from her pocket and drank down her daily dose of the tonic Vasudev delivered to her, lest she too be burned passing through the Fire. Then she walked slowly into it. When she reemerged some time later, she carried the souls of two babies in her arms and the older children walked behind her in a row like ducklings. Silently, they followed her out of Hell.

And far away in the mountains of Kashmir, the rescuers, on the very verge of giving up, unearthed a pocket of air and pulled twenty-two children out of the rubble alive.

It was a miracle.

· T W O ·

The Curse

At the British parties in Jaipur, gossip swirled wild on eddies of whiskeyed breath. The old bitch was a popular topic of it. It was generally agreed that she had been in India too long. It had 'gotten to her.' She spoke the native tongue, and not just Hindustani but also Rajasthani and a touch of Gujarati, and she had even been heard to haggle once in Persian! It suggested to the British a grubby intimacy with the place, as if she took India into her very mouth and *tasted* it, like a lover's fingers. It was indecent.

And if that wasn't bad enough, she ate mangoes in the bazaar with the natives, juice dribbling down her chin, and was said to imbibe a tonic prepared for her daily by a dreadful little man with a burn scar over half his face. She touched beggars and had even been seen carrying rag-swaddled infants home with her in her arms. It was rumored that her handsome factotum had been one such baby, which in itself bespoke a lifetime in this land – a lifetime of rescued beggar babes grown to manhood.

He was always at her side, lordly as a raja and unsmiling as an assassin, with a dangerous gleam in his eye and odd bulges about his tailored suits that hinted at concealed knives. Plenty of whispers went round town about him – that he could speak with tigers, that he had a forked tail he wore tucked down one trouser leg (the left), that he had been seen crossing a street without his shadow, and that he would do anything for the old bitch. Even the most shameless of gossips can inadvertently hit upon truths. He *would* do anything for her, and had done, many times.

Pranjivan was his name, which meant 'life,' and Estella had given him both: his name *and* his life. She had carried him out of the Fire in her arms when he was a tiny brown child too young to follow on his own two feet. He alone knew all her secrets, and aside from his household duties, he spied for her. He sent out his shadow across the land – she had taught him how when he was a boy – and he maintained detailed lists of the wicked. He helped Estella decide who would die, in order that children might live. And when she emerged from Hell each day through a trapdoor in the shade of a massive peepal tree, he was there waiting for her with the rickshaw men, ready to take her home.

On the day of the earthquake, he knew something was wrong as soon as she came up blinking into the light of day. 'What is it, Memsahib?' he asked.

'Take me to the Agent's Residence,' she said quietly, and he did.

Jaipur was a Rajput kingdom ruled by warrior princes, not a part of the British Empire. There were no officious governors or magistrates here, only the Political Agent, a mustachioed former cavalryman whose military career had come to an end when he lost an arm to a tigress in the Himalayas. Now he had to hold the reins in his teeth when he hunted jackal with the native princes, which was one of his primary duties, and for which service he was rewarded with a palatial home and a small army of servants. He even kept a hookah-burda just to light his pipe.

When Estella appeared uninvited at his gate, the party was in full swing. It was a christening for the Agent's third daughter, but it looked like any other party – bright gowns billowing in a garden, gentlemen lolling about with drinks sweating in their big, hot hands. There was a table laden with gifts, and there was a pink iced cake, but the baby's bassinet seemed like an afterthought at the edge of things, and the baby within lay silent and composed, gazing up at the fringe of neem trees with solemn gray eyes.

'What's the old bitch doing here?' murmured the Political Agent to his wife, and they both cringed. At the best of times Estella had a way of robbing them of amusement at their own vapid talk, and she looked particularly grim on this occasion. The usually neat coils of her silver hair were frayed from the drafts of hellfire she had passed through, and her heart was heavy with the curse she had come to deliver.

She went straight to the bassinet and looked down at the pretty baby. Silence fell over the merrymakers. It struck them all like a scene from a fairy tale, and Estella a witch come to spoil their fun. 'She looks like a madwoman,' someone whispered. Estella didn't even look up. She reached toward the baby, and the baby grasped her finger and smiled up at her.

Estella's heart clenched. She couldn't change her mind. Twenty-two children in Kashmir *lived* and Vasudev wouldn't hesitate to take them back again; he was no doubt dreaming up awful accidents at this very moment. So she did what she had come to do. She said, 'I curse this child with the most beautiful voice ever to slip from human lips.' She looked up and peered around at the partygoers. Their faces were flushed with laughter, with liquor. They seemed to be waiting for her to continue, so she did. 'But take care that you never hear it. Anyone who does shall fall down dead on the spot. From this moment forward, any sound this child utters will *kill.*'

There were gasps across the garden, and then a titter of incredulous laughter. Someone cried out, 'A curse! How rare!'

'Capital fun!'

'It's too, too divine!'

Estella stared at them. Delight gleamed in their eyes. They didn't believe her. Of course they didn't. Her Majesty's subjects didn't go around believing things willy-nilly. But whether they believed it or not, the curse was as real as the heat, and soon they would know it.

How soon?

Estella's finger was still caught in the girl's tiny fist – she'd never ceased to marvel at the strength of a baby's grip – and she looked back down into those gray eyes. She was a lovely little thing, this child. Estella had never had a baby of her own, her husband had died so young. In the darkness of grief in the days after his death, she'd hoped ferociously that there might be a baby – that something of him might be arranging itself within her even as she followed his coffin to the cemetery. But it was not to be. She had been left alone, and she had also been left *empty.*

A breeze stirred the trees and the baby smiled again. She looked as if she might coo, and Estella felt suddenly that her own death was perched upon her shoulder like a bird. How easy to die, she thought, and how fitting, if she were to be the first victim of this curse . . . the first victim of this child, whom at the behest of a demon she had just turned into a murderer. For, as surely as twenty-two children in Kashmir *lived*, people in Jaipur would *die.*

But not yet. Vasudev had his curses, but Estella was not without power of her own. Before the Political Agent's wife could sweep over and scoop up her child, Estella leaned down, pressed her fingertip gently but firmly to the baby's lips and whispered, 'You will stay silent, won't you, little thing? Until you are old enough to understand the curse, your voice will be as a bird in a cage.'

And so it was.

Year by year the girl grew up. Queen Victoria died. Black rats aboard steamships carried plague from China to India. Millions died. Estella and Vasudev were kept very busy. The Great War began with a shot. The Germans used poison gas first, but the British followed suit. They were so ashamed of themselves they forbade the very soldiers who carried the chlorine canisters from uttering the word 'gas.' Millions died. In India, Vasudev's curses mostly came to their fruition. Among their victims were a child in Chittagong who went fleetingly invisible every time she sneezed, and a Punjabi princeling who crowed like a cockerel at dawn.

But through some remarkable depth of will, the gray-eyed daughter of the Agent of Jaipur held her own curse in a curious limbo, and after more than seventeen years, the British still had no reason to believe in it.

Vasudev chafed and swore. 'It's not fair, you meddling with the servants!' he hissed to Estella, his face flushing in fury so that its two halves nearly matched crimson. 'You haven't let things take their natural course!'

'Natural course?' Estella repeated, giving him a flat look. 'There are no curses in the "natural course." You've had every opportunity to influence the Agent's servants too, Vasudev. You spend enough time spying in the garden there.'

The demon gave her a sour look but said nothing. What could he say? That that damned Pranjivan had taken unfair advantage of his broad shoulders and flashing white teeth to sway the girl's servants? That the factotum was too damned handsome, and an ugly little demon hadn't a chance at a game like that? It was true, but he wouldn't say it. Even demons have some dignity. The truth was, Estella had won – *so far*. First that trick of whispering the girl silent until she was old enough to understand the curse, and now this. The servants believed Pranjivan, damned handsome beggar, and the girl believed the servants. In that raucous palace of singing sisters, she lived her life butterfly-silent, never giving so much as a laugh out loud. When Vasudev spied on her in the garden, he saw a deep sadness in her, a dreamy wistfulness, but he never saw her test the curse, not even on a beetle or an ant. It was inhuman. The girl wasn't normal!

That one unfulfilled curse was the single blemish on Vasudev's joy when he guessed that the old bitch was dying.

Estella had been old for a long time, and sometimes the demon had feared that she would never die, that he would be hamstrung by her human sensibilities forever. But now she was fading. Growing papery. Pain became plain in every furrow of her face and in the way she moved gingerly down the onyx tunnels to their morning meetings. She was dying at last! Vasudev wanted to gloat, but the curse restrained him. It was unthinkable he shouldn't have the satisfaction of it while the old bitch was still alive to suffer from it!

He sat opposite Estella and drummed his fingers on the table, unable to triumph at her pain and pallor. Furiously he wondered how he might finally tip the balance. How he might make the girl speak at last.

He had no way of knowing, as he scowled and muttered, that at that very moment a soldier on a train from Bombay was discovering a lost diary wedged between the seat and the wall, and not just any lost diary, but the lost diary of the cursed girl herself. And even as that train wended its way toward Jaipur, the soldier was flipping it open to the first page.

Some would assert that Providence was at work, shaking out its pockets in Humanity's lap. Others would argue for that mindless choreographer, Chance. Either way it was a simple thing: A lost diary fell into the hands of a soul-sick war hero on a train from Bombay to Jaipur just when he'd grown tired of the scenery and needed something to keep his thoughts from the minefield of his wretched memories.

In such mild ways is the groundwork laid for first kisses and ruined lives.

FOUR

The Soldier

The soldier's name was James Dorsey, and he had dropped his lighter down between the seat and the wall of the compartment. It was the lighter his friend Gaffney had told him to take off his corpse if he became a corpse, and then he had. Six hundred thousand men had died at the Somme, but James had not. What remained of his regiment had been torn apart in the Second Marne, and again, somehow, James had survived. He'd joined the Foreign Office after the War and come to India for another try at death – a more interesting one than mortars and gas, perhaps. Here among the tigers and the dacoits' long knives there were many to choose from, not the least of them the marvelous fevers with names like exotic flowers.

Digging out the dropped lighter, James found the diary wedged down between the seat and the wall and he fished it out too. It was bound in floral linen and filled with girlish script. 'The secrets of a blushing maiden,' he quipped with a smile that brought his dimples out, and he flipped it right open with no scruple to preserving the maidenly modesty of its writer. Indeed, he expected none. He had endured his sea voyage in the company of the 'fishing fleet' – English ladies hying themselves to India to catch husbands – and he felt as if he had barely escaped being drugged and dragged to the altar. He thought he knew the character of English girls in India, and surely this diary would be more of the same.

Tucking Gaffney's lighter back into his pocket, James began to read.

His smile wavered. It clung for a time in disbelief and then fell away in stages. The little book did indeed hold the secrets of a blushing maiden, but they weren't the sort of secrets he'd expected, and by the time his train arrived in Jaipur, James had read the diary through twice and found himself – against all expectation – to be half in love with its writer.

That was ridiculous, of course. Certainly a man couldn't fall in love with cursive on a page, could he? He scanned the inside covers of the little book for some hint of the girl's identity but found no name.

So, a mystery.

He held the book tenderly as he stepped off the train and into his new life, and later, in his lodgings, he read it a third time, mining it for clues as to who the girl might be. There was enough to suggest she had lived in Jaipur, though whether she still did was uncertain. The diary had been lost on a train, after all. It occurred to him she might be gone. Absurdly, the thought left him desolate. He chided himself that she was only a stranger.

But she wasn't, really. She was all here, in this book. Not her name, and not her face, but *she* was here, and absurd or not, he thought he *might* actually love her.

If she was in Jaipur, he vowed, he would find her.

He didn't have long to wait. It was only his second day in the city when he was invited to a garden party at the Agent's Residence.

The upper echelons of the Indian Civil Service were known as the 'heaven-born,' and when James saw the legion of white-turbaned servants bearing trays of colored sweets and cocktails among the fantastical banyan trees and the overlush vine flowers, he began to see why. In England, bureaucrats could never have lived like this, like little kings with monkeys on leashes and stables full of fine hunting horses. He smiled at his new colleagues, but behind his smile he was thinking how these men had been tipping back gin while other, better men had been holding in their entrails with both hands. His fingers went automatically to Gaffney's lighter in his pocket.

All of James's childhood friends had died in the War. Every single one. James often wondered at the chain of flukes it must have taken to bring him through with his own life and limbs intact. Once, he might have believed it to be the work of Providence, but it seemed to him now that to thank God for his life would be to suggest God had shrugged off all the others, flicked them away like cigarette butts by the thousands, and that seemed like abominable conceit. James Dorsey took no credit for being alive. His higher power these days was Chance.

He was distracted from his grim thoughts when he heard a raspy voice over his left shoulder say, 'That one, at the piano, that's the girl the old bitch cursed. Damned good fun!'

His cursed girl! James's first impulse was to turn to look but he stopped himself. He didn't like that raspy voice. It had a lecherous sneer about it, and he didn't want his first glimpse of the girl to come at the end of a lecher's pointing finger. He held himself still, his back to the conversation and the piano. He heard the music, though, and became suddenly alert to it.

He had a good ear, and even in the din of high, thin laughter and meaty guffaws he could tell the pianist was extraordinary. Again, he almost turned, but stopped himself and went on listening, imagining what she looked like, trying to conjure a face from the exquisite notes that flowed from her fingers. Delicate, he guessed, but passionate. He felt certain her hair would be dark, and whimsically he imagined freckles. He smiled. It had been a long time since he had savored anticipation like this. Mostly in the past years the things he'd anticipated had been heart-stopping, vicious things like death-wish dashes from one trench to the next.

While the notes of a Chopin sonata drifted through the garden, he waited and imagined, and behind him, the gossip ensued.

'Cursed?' asked a brassy female voice.

'She's going to be the death of us all,' came the reply in a low, ominous whisper such as children affect to tell ghost stories by candlelight.

The woman laughed and asked skeptically, *'Her?'*

'I know, I know. She seems an unlikely instrument of doom, but so it is. It happened at her christening. The old bitch – the emerald miner's widow, you've heard about her? – stood over her frilled bassinet and said the lass would slay us all . . . not with knives, mind you, or with poison in our rum or asps in our beds, not by mutiny or pistol or any other means you might conjure for killing, but with a very queer murder weapon indeed. You see, that little lady will slay us with . . .' – he paused for effect – '. . . her *voice.*'

This was not news to James, who had read the girl's diary, but he heard a derisive snort of laughter from the woman. 'Her *voice?* Whatever do you mean?' she asked.

Slowly, careful to keep the piano out of his line of sight, James turned to the gossipmongers. The lecher was a white-bearded fellow and the woman had a horsey, well-bred face. They were craning their necks to see across the garden, and there was a leer in the man's eyes as he darted out his pink tongue to wet his lips. With great restraint, James did not follow his lewd gaze to the piano.

'Simply this,' the lecher explained to the woman. 'The old bitch pronounced that when the girl speaks, all within earshot shall drop down dead.'

'Ha-ha! You lot are still living, I see. It must have been a good joke when she spoke her first words – bit of a flinch all around?'

'Yes, well, I suppose there *will* be. You see, she has never yet uttered a single sound.'

'What? *Ever?* Not even as a baby?'

'Not after the christening. Not a peep. Damnedest thing.'

An ominous silence was left to hang there. The heat felt carnivorous. The lecher drained his drink and looked for more. The ice was running low. There was never enough ice. British hands looked swollen clutching their cocktails. There was in the air always the subtle stench of overripe fruit. For years after these British had returned to their dainty island, when they smelled this soft decay, they would think of fevers and legless beggars, and sad elephants wandering down lanes.

'And has she *really* never made a sound?' the horsey woman murmured.

'Nary a sigh nor a snort of indignation,' said the girl's own mother, joining them and watching her daughter as if she were a monkey brought to entertain them. '*She* believes the curse. I think the servants convinced her of it. Always *whispering*. Indians and their nonsense!'

'A bit eerie though, isn't it?' the woman said uneasily. She was new to India, and she was finding that here in this wild land, strange twinges of *belief* had a way of intruding into one's cultured *disbelief*, like trick cards in a deck to be drawn at random. In India, sometimes, one could accidentally believe the oddest things. 'Perhaps she's just mute,' she suggested hopefully.

'Perhaps,' allowed the mother, her eyes twinkling with merry mischief as she said in a baleful voice, 'Who knows, though. Perhaps it's all true. If you'd like to find out, I'll encourage her to sing us an aria. Her sisters have been practicing "Una voce poca fa" and she must surely have the words by heart.'

'Damn me,' said her husband, the one-armed Agent of Jaipur himself. 'I'm sure even the servants and the mynah birds have the words by heart. The girls never stop wailing that bloody thing.'

'Wailing! Gerald, hush!' She batted at him with her hand and the others laughed. 'The girls must have their culture!'

'Culture!' the Agent hooted. Catching sight of James, he said with a conspiratorial wink, 'Girl's got the right idea in my book. Nothing wrong with a silent woman, eh?'

James forced himself to smile. He doubted his smile could conceal his loathing of these people, but they didn't seem to notice it. After a moment he drifted away from them and wandered at the edge of the garden. He knew by the music – Liszt now – that the girl was still at the piano, and he wanted to cleanse the gossip from his mind before he finally let himself see her. He breathed the scent of a strange lily and fingered some broad waxen leaves. He watched a beetle's progress across a flagstone, and when he could stand it no longer, he turned on his heel and looked to the piano.

And there she was.

Her composure marked her out at once from the women around her, who laughed too loudly with their heads thrown back. Her back was straight, her neck white. Her hair, upswept, was the color of dark chocolate. She was turned away from him so James began to move through the crowd, ignoring the coy murmurs of other girls as he went.

He wended his way round to the foot of the grand piano and the girl was revealed to him. Her face, as he had known it would be, was perfect. It was heart-shaped and delicate and flushed with the exertions of her passionate playing. Her eyes were downcast, their color still a mystery. James was strangely moved to see that she did indeed have freckles, as he had imagined. They were as fine as a sift of cinnamon, and he found himself wanting to count them, to lie with her in a sunny patch of garden and touch them one by one, tracing the contours of her cheek, letting his finger drift down to her lips. . . . He saw she was biting her lip.

Drinking in his first close sight of her, James already knew her better than any of these others did. He knew from her diary that if she was biting her lip, it meant she was having one of her bad days.

He had imagined himself, fancifully, to be half in love with the writer of the mysterious diary, but now, seeing her, that vague fancy was swept away by the exhilaration of *actually* falling in love with her, not by halves, but fully and profoundly. His heartbeat pulsed in his hands with the desire to reach out and touch her.

She looked up suddenly and saw him. She saw the naked look in his eyes and her fingers faltered on the keys. The jarring of the music turned all heads and everyone at the party witnessed that first fused stare. James couldn't look away from her. Her eyes were pale gray and they were lonely, and haunted, and hungry. She slowly released her lower lip from between her teeth as she stared back at him.

She was feeling, under the vivid gaze of this soldier, that she had stepped out of a fog and been seen clearly for the first time.

· FIVE ·

The Caged Bird

In her diary she had written:

Most days I believe in the curse with all my heart. I believe that I might kill with no more effort than it takes others to sing or pray. Those days are easy. My voice sleeps and I have no terrible impulses to speak. But some days I wake with doubts and worse, spite, and every moment speech trembles on my lips so that I have to bite them. I look at the faces all around me, my parents, that horrid old chaplain, all the others with that tippling flush in their cheeks too early in the day, and I think I will burst into song just to see the flash of terror in their eyes before we know, all of us and at last, if it is true or not. If I can kill them all with a word.

Those are the bad days.

So far, I have managed to forbear and doubtless I will go on forbearing. But sometimes when they treat me like an idiot child, talking loud and in short sentences, with that smug sense of their own charity — how good they are, to speak to the idiot girl! — I can't help but amuse myself deliberating, if I were to kill them with a word, what should that word be? Hello? Listen? Oops? But I rather think it wouldn't be a

word at all, but a song, that they might hear the voice I sacri-
fice for their sake every single day.

I am always sick with guilt after such wicked thoughts,
and the guilt drives the wickedness out.

Her name was Anamique, after a Flemish soprano her mother
had heard sing the role of Isolde once at Bayreuth. Anamique had
been singing Isolde in her head since she was twelve and her mother
had ordered the libretto for her older daughters' singing lessons.
Inside herself, where she sang, Anamique's voice was far more beautiful than her sisters' voices, but she was the only one who knew it.
She was the only one who would *ever* know it.

Years of warnings had built up in her. Her ayah believed the
curse and so did the rest of the servants, even the stern old Rajput
whose job it had been to guide her around the garden on her pony,
Mackerel, when she was small. The servants had always implored
her to keep silent, and they prevailed. Even while her mother commanded her to speak, her ayah was there whispering in Rajasthani in
her other ear, 'Hush, my pearl, keep quiet. You must keep your voice
in its cage, like a beautiful bird. If you let it out, it will kill us all.'

Anamique believed her. One couldn't help believing things
whispered in Rajasthani.

To her family, she wrote notes on a small tablet she carried
always with her, though her mother often disdained to read them, as
it would have required putting on her spectacles, which she took
great pains never to do.

For the servants, who were illiterate, Anamique developed an
elaborate language of gestures that almost looked like dance when
shaped by her graceful hands. And when they spoke to her – bless

them – they didn't raise their voices as if she were deaf, or speak slowly as if she were dim-witted.

Because of her silence, Anamique had not been sent to school in England like her sisters and all the other British children, but had spent her whole life in India, and most of that with the servants. There was more of India in her than of that far green isle she had rarely seen. She played the vina as well as she played the piano, and she knew all the Hindu gods by name. She had ridden a camel in the Thar Desert, scooped rice into a saddhu's bowl, and been lifted by an elephant's trunk to gather figs from the high branches. She had even gone back to her ayah's dusty village for festivals and slept on a string charpoy with the native children, nestled together like spoons. The voice that was full within her not only sang full lyric soprano but could chant the Vedas, and yet she bit her lip and played accompaniment to her sisters' unremarkable singing.

As her ayah instructed, she kept her own voice like a bird in a cage. She imagined it as a willful songbird with a puffed breast, its feathers gray like her eyes, with a flash of peacock blue at the neck, and the cage as an ornate prison of rusted scrollwork with a little latched door that she never dared open. Sometimes the urge to do so was nearly overpowering.

She was playing piano for her sisters one afternoon a few days after the garden party when a parcel was delivered for her. The chaprassi brought it to her and Anamique ceased playing at once so that her eldest sister's voice was left stranded in the air. 'Ana!' Rosie scolded, but Anamique paid her no heed. Nothing had ever been delivered just for her before. She scraped back the piano bench and took the twine-tied parcel out into the garden where she opened it and slid her diary out. Stunned, she clasped it to her chest. She had thought it lost forever! Her relief bled into agitation, though, as she began to think of someone finding it, *reading* it, as they must have done to know to deliver it here. Her heartbeat quickened as she opened the little book and saw a letter tucked inside it. With trembling fingers she unfolded it and read:

When I was a boy, it was my job to slice the heels off the new loaves and throw them in the woodstove to feed the imp my mum said lived in the fire, to forestall him burning down our cottage out of spite. He was a hungry imp, she said, but I was a hungry boy and I ate those heels myself when she looked away, and that poor imp might've starved but our cottage never burned, and maybe I grew taller for the extra bread.

And I was tasked more than once to go and drown the May kittens in the pond, as my gran said cats born in that unlucky month suffocated babes in their cradles and invited snakes into the house. But I never killed a kitten in my life and only hid them and brought them cream when I could. And never did a baby die from my failure to murder kittens, nor a snake cross our threshold but that I brought it there myself in the pocket of my own short pants.

And I have fought on the plains of France where evil fifinelle spirits, they say, tickle gunners and make their shells go astray. And though I manned a howitzer myself and sent many shells arcing into the night, I never felt their tickle on my neck. Maybe the fifinelles fought for our side and only beleaguered the Germans, and maybe a shell went astray by their ministrations that would have been meant for me.

94

Or maybe all that's done in the world is done by men and chance, and omens are only fears, and curses are only fancies. I never saw God save a kitten or fill a boy's belly with bread, and I never met him on the battlefield passing out gas masks to the men. And if he can't be troubled to catch some bullets in his fists, and if he won't reach down to grab a mountain and keep it from crumbling away, and if he forgets to send the rains one year and millions die of hunger, is it likely he's bothering himself cursing one beautiful girl in Jaipur?

Maybe he's sitting somewhere right now knitting up Providence like homespun, but I've seen too much blood to ever trust his cloth. I would sooner trust to a song from your lips than to Providence, though I've seen no proof of either one. When the day comes that you finally sing, I hope I shall be in the audience. In truth, I hope I might be the only member of your audience, that I might hoard all your words for myself. I believe I had forgotten about beauty until I saw you, and now I'm greedy for it, like the boy I was once, recklessly eating all the imp's portion of bread.

Yours, enchanted, James Dorsey

Anamique remembered the way the handsome soldier had stared at her in the garden, the way he had *seen* her, and she flushed and had to bite her lip. She tucked the letter back into her diary but a moment later took it out and read it again. And again.

She passed the night restlessly, waking from vivid dreams of singing to lie wide-eyed in the dark with a pounding heart, listening for any trace of her voice lingering in the air. Once she even went to her sister's door and strained to hear her breathing and be sure her voice hadn't escaped in her sleep and slain the whole household. Finally, afraid to close her eyes, she composed a reply to the letter. It was simply a quotation from Kipling and it read:

East of Suez, some hold, the direct control of Providence ceases; man being there handed over to the power of the Gods and Devils of Asia, and the Church of England Providence only exercising an occasional and modified supervision in the case of Englishmen.

After breakfast she gave it to the chaprassi to deliver.

James laughed when he read it, a bright, surprised burst of a laugh. He wrote to her again, fabulating a means by which, he outrageously claimed, the devils of India might easily be outwitted by leaving out saucers of sherry overnight for their spies, the wall lizards, who would grow tipsy and forget to carry their mission reports back to Hell.

This too the chaprassi duly delivered, and Anamique wrote back again the same day to tell him how her ayah practiced *gowli shastra*, the art of reading the stripes and scamperings of wall lizards for omens. She added, shyly, that she had been to an astrologer once in the bazaar. She had never told anyone that, and James wondered in his reply what fortune had been foretold for her, and had it mentioned a soldier, by chance?

For days in a row they continued in this way, and slowly they discovered each other. The letters grew longer and Anamique's gray eyes lost a bit of the haunted shadow James had seen in them, and James's heart began to lift itself, step by step, out of the swamp of mud and ghosts in which it had been steeping since France.

The First Touch

The second time they saw each other was at a musical eve-ning arranged by Anamique's mother. She routinely invited the unmarried young men over for a spot of light opera to amuse her daughters, and James was handsome, and he was a war hero, and to top it all off he turned out to have a glorious tenor voice. The one thing that kept him from becoming a new favorite among the memsahibs was his irredeemable habit of looking only at Anamique while he sang.

The others all remembered that stare in the garden, and they could see now in the look that passed between the two that some-thing was already under way. A bridge begun at both ends, reaching toward the place in the middle where they could rest against each other and find completion.

James cajoled an old missionary's wife to take a turn at the piano at the end of the evening, so he might have the chance to dance with Anamique. They touched for the first time, first deli-cately and decorously, fingertips to waist and hand to shoulder in the pose of the dance. But by and by James's lips brushed softly against Anamique's earlobe as he whispered something to her. She blushed furiously at the intimate touch, and a look of wistfulness and hope came into her eyes.

'I love you,' he had whispered, and it seemed to him as she pressed her lips together, that she was imagining whispering it back.

She *was* imagining it. She thought she could *taste* the words, all ginger and chili and sugar, fiery and sweet, and she held them in her mouth like candies. It would take more time than this to coax them from her, but something began to happen at that moment. An idea fell like a seed, and over the next weeks it went on growing like a fig vine, lush and conquering, twining round her old beliefs and covering them in new growth until they were as invisible as a tiger in a thicket – and just as deadly.

There were more musical evenings and more letters, furtive hand-holding at dinner, duets at the piano, more dancing, more whispers in her ear that raised goose bumps on Anamique's neck and sent shivers down her spine. They were never alone, but may as well have been, the way they looked only at each other. Sitting apart from the crowd at whatever party or gathering they were at, James spoke, and Anamique wrote on her tablet small notes that James saved and kept with her letters. She even began to teach him some of the simpler signs of her gesture language, such as those for 'thirsty' and 'dance.' He asked her, eyes merry, how to sign 'I love you,' just so he would recognize it if she ever gestured it to him, and, blushing, she showed him.

Anamique grew radiant. Other men began to wonder why it had taken that damned James Dorsey to make them see that, silent or not, Anamique was quite the loveliest creature in Jaipur, if not all of India. None of them bothered to court her, though; they couldn't even catch her eye, and she demurred from dancing with anyone but James.

And while they danced, James whispered to her. He urged her to sing for him, to tell him that she loved him. 'How can I ever believe it,' he asked, his brown eyes pleading, 'unless you tell me so yourself?' He knew about the bird in the cage, and he imagined it languishing there like a sad animal in a roadside menagerie. 'Birds shouldn't be kept in cages,' he told her, his lips warm against her ear. 'They should fly.'

By and by Anamique formed a resolution: If James asked her to marry him, she would answer him. The first word she would ever speak aloud would be *yes*.

SEVEN

The Gloating Demon

Crouched in the garden muttering, Vasudev saw the light in Anamique's eyes and gave a loathsome gloating chuckle. The girl was in love! Nothing could scatter caution like love. Nothing could turn a girl silly half so fast as a handsome soldier whispering in her ear! And a soldier begging her *to talk*, no less! It was so perfect it almost made Vasudev believe in Providence, but he knew the way the cogs worked and whirred in the winding up and down of human lives. Gods though there might be, they cared little for the minutiae. If an English soldier had lived through the bloodiest war the world had ever known and made his way half around the planet to fall in love with this particular girl and goad her into fulfilling her curse, well, Vasudev had only that mad bastard Chance to thank for it, and he did.

It came in the nick of time too. The old bitch wouldn't last much longer. Vasudev gave her a week at the most. He chuckled again. Estella had missed their tea that morning for the first time ever. He had waited for her in Hell, his smile widening with each passing moment that didn't bring her tall, spare silhouette down the black tunnel.

He had her tonic in his pocket now, and went whistling up to her ornate, filigreed palace to deliver it. 'Good day to you!' he cried when Pranjivan opened the door to him. With feigned solicitude Vasudev asked, 'Is Memsahib feeling unwell today?'

Pranjivan gave him his customary stony stare and said, 'Memsahib is very busy and sends word she will come tomorrow at the usual time.'

Vasudev laughed out loud. 'She hasn't missed a day's descent to Hell since Yama foisted her on me. Not for any illness, not for anything! Busy? My teeth, Pranjivan, lying beggar that you are. If she isn't dying, she'd better come tell me so herself.'

Pranjivan didn't even blink. 'Have you brought Memsahib's tonic?' he asked.

What Vasudev resented most about the factotum was his stolidness. Even Estella could be made to wince and scowl, but Pranjivan, never. His face may as well have been cast in an expressionless mold. The demon found it extremely unrewarding. Reluctantly he produced the flask and handed it over. 'Not that she'll need it,' he said. 'I imagine the next time I see dear Estella in Hell it will be her soul alone, drawn like a moth to the flames, just like any other pathetic human.'

Pranjivan started to shut the door in Vasudev's face and the demon blurted, 'And I wager she'll have a whole lot of British company on her way, do you hear me? I'll see that curse through yet!'

The door snicked shut. Vasudev stamped his foot and hollered, 'That girl's going to speak! Do you hear me? Any time now her voice is going to burst out of her like a tornado and I'm going to win! She's in love, Pranjivan old devil! Do you hear? A girl will do crazy things for love. Just ask Estella – *she* went to *Hell* for it!'

There was no answer from within and Vasudev was left standing at the servants' entrance, breathing fast through gritted teeth. 'Damn

Pranjivan,' he muttered, giving up and going away, trying to console himself by dreaming up grim deaths for the beggar once Estella was finally dead and not there to protect him. *Something painful,* he thought.

Something excruciating.

EIGHT

The Stolen Shadow

Anamique's eighteenth birthday party was the following evening. In his rooms, James slid a small velvet ring box into his pocket, put on his dinner jacket, and took a deep breath. He couldn't afford much in the way of a diamond, much as he couldn't really afford to support a wife, especially a privileged heaven-born daughter like Anamique. It was madness, surely, but of all the madness he had known, it was the sweetest. He patted his pocket and set out.

He had just bought flowers and was walking past the Palace of the Winds when a man loomed up before him, tall, Indian, severe. For a moment James thought he must be a cutthroat, he had such a look of intensity – almost savagery – in his eyes, but then he recognized him by his fine English suit. Here was the factotum of the widow called 'the old bitch,' the one who had filled Anamique's head with fear and nonsense and blighted her young life with silence.

'What do you want, man?' James asked him, drawing himself up to his full height, which, he was pleased to see, was a bit taller than the Indian's.

'Do you love the girl?' Pranjivan asked.

'It's no business of yours,' said James, his voice dropping to a growl.

'If you love her, you can love her silence too.'

'Love her *silence*? What is this? Some kind of a game?'

'It is a game, but not a funny one. It's a demon's game, and if you encourage the girl to speak, you encourage her to kill you, and the demon wins. I especially wish the demon not to win.'

'Demon?' James said. 'Are you mad? There are no demons. There are no curses. There are only vicious jokes and vile people, tormenting an innocent girl!'

Pranjivan shook his head and said, 'Are you really so certain? Would you look at a rock in a field and claim no cobra lies beneath it because you can't see it?'

'And what is it I can't see? Demons?'

'You can see demons.'

James looked around him at the throng of camels and rick-shaws and stern turbaned men with twirled mustaches. He cocked an eyebrow at Pranjivan, who smiled a thin smile and said, 'There are none nearby just now.'

'Of course not. Look, I'll just be on my way. I don't have time for your mythology today.' James stepped around Pranjivan and continued down the avenue.

Pranjivan fell into step beside him. 'Oh? Why is that? What happens today?'

James gave him a dark glance but didn't answer. In his pocket, his hand curled around the little velvet box.

'From what I hear,' said Pranjivan, 'she would be devastated if she killed you. For her sake, I wish that not to happen.'

'How good of you.'

'If you wish to protect her—'

'I wish to *marry* her,' said James, turning to face him.

'So marry her,' said Pranjivan in a low, urgent voice. 'But *believe.* The world goes down deeper than you know, Englishman. There *are* cobras under the rocks, and there *are* curses.'

The urgency in the Indian's voice perplexed James. He might be mad, but he was certainly sincere. What was this all about? The strength of James's certainty weakened just a little.

Pranjivan went on. 'She mustn't speak. Believe it. Believe there is more to the world than what your own eyes have seen.' Then he nodded his head in a sharp farewell and crossed the avenue to a waiting rickshaw. James watched him go. He saw him climb in, and he saw the rickshaw men gather up their poles, but before they could start off, a spidery hand reached out from within the shadows of the contraption and the men halted.

The street was banded with shadows slung low and long by the setting sun, and James couldn't make out the second figure in the rickshaw until she sat forward. It seemed to cost her a great effort to move that little bit, and when her face came into the light, James saw Estella. She looked very ill. Her face was pinched and sallow, but her eyes burned with a fearsome intensity. James felt a shiver pass through him as she looked straight at him.

'What does she want?' he wondered. Uneasy, he started walking toward her but he hadn't gone more than a few steps when the old bitch reached her hand out of the rickshaw and, in a sudden startling motion, snatched James's shadow away.

He faltered and stared at his feet, then up at the rickshaw, then back at his feet. What had he just seen? The old bitch had reached out one frail hand, clutched it suddenly into a fist, and pulled – and James's long thin shadow had gone taut before him, then disengaged from his feet and scudded over the cobbles to disappear into the shadowy rickshaw. He almost thought he had *felt it* pull free. A smile quavered at the corners of his lips and he wanted to laugh at the absurdity of it.

But when a box-wallah paused beside him to reshoulder his burden before crossing the street, James couldn't help but see the man's shadow splayed out thick and dark over the cobbles and beside it . . . nothing. James cast no shadow at all.

The old bitch slumped wearily back in her seat and Pranjivan gave James a long look before ordering the rickshaw runners to move off. An incredulous laugh burst from James's lips as he thought of calling out, 'Stop! Thief!' He turned in a circle to see if anyone had been watching, but the street sweepers and lamplighters were all going about their own business, and the rickshaw soon faded into the gloom.

James resumed his walk toward the Agent's Residence with a fervor of thoughts clashing in his mind. He didn't *believe* in magic and demons. He believed in day and night, endurance and fury, cold mud and loneliness and the speed with which blood leaves the body. He also believed in miserable, defiant hope and the way the shape of the girl you love can fill your arms like an eidolon when you dream about dancing with her.

But whether he believed it or not, his shadow was . . . *missing*. With each person he passed he was forced to acknowledge its absence in stark contrast to the many quick shadows slipping by on the street. By the time he reached the gates of the Residence, he had begun to feel as if a neat slit had been opened in the lining of reason, letting madness sidle in.

'Sahib!' a little street boy cried, running up to him.

'Yes, little man? What is it?'

'The old memsahib, she say give you this, Sahib,' the child told him breathlessly, tossing something at James's chest so he had to catch it. It was a little parcel of brown paper, and as the boy ran off, James unfolded it. It was weightless; it seemed empty, but as it fell open, a mass of darkness hit the ground at James's feet, dark and quick as paint splashed from a bucket. It was his shadow, and it was crisp beneath the lamps of the Agent's gates now, as if it had never been gone. Inside the little parcel, on the brown paper, was scrawled one word. *Believe.*

James's soul trembled, just a little.

Inside, Anamique was watching for James. A pianist had been hired for the evening so that she might not have to entertain at her own party, and the fellow was playing a rowdy ragtime tune. Others were dancing and laughing, but for Anamique the party wouldn't begin until James arrived. She looked in a mirror and saw a strange girl looking out. She smiled. She'd had her hair bobbed. Her sisters had sculpted it into finger waves and it looked glossy and sleek against her cheeks. She wasn't a girl anymore, and she wasn't wearing a girl's gown either. She wore a jazzy shimmering shift that fell to mid-calf, and in her stockings and strappy shoes her ankles felt naked. Her shoulders were bare too and she felt daring and sultry and alive.

She saw James reflected in the mirror and she turned. He'd just come in and was looking for her. She watched mischievously as his eyes swept the room, passing over her twice before finally fixing on her face with a flash of surprise. His startled brown eyes dropped to her shoulders, then down to her ankles and darted quickly back up to her face as a blush overspread his cheeks. He stood immobile for a moment, clutching a bouquet of flowers, before crossing the room to her in a rush.

'Ana . . .' he breathed. 'You look . . . ravishing . . .' He was flustered, and couldn't keep his eyes from straying down to her white shoulders. Anamique wanted to dance with him so he would touch her. She wanted him to cup her shoulders with both hands and whisper in her ear, close, his lips touching her so her whole body would shiver like flower petals in a breeze. She wanted him to kiss her. Looking up into his eyes and seeing the radiance in them, seeing *the future* in them, she was so full of happiness she thought she might burst. She had to bite her lip to keep from singing.

A flicker of anxiety passed through James's eyes when she bit her lip. She laid her hand on his arm and looked up at him, silently asking with her eyes, 'What is it?'

Whatever it was, he shook it off. 'Look at me, stammering like a fool! You've taken my breath away, Ana, my beautiful girl. I haven't even told you happy birthday yet! Well, happy birthday. Now dance with me!'

He took her hand and led her to the dance floor, and all evening long they danced and danced. Around them the party happened. There were streamers stretched over their heads, and people drank and gossiped, and khitmutgars moved among them with trays of cakes, but Anamique didn't pay attention to any of it. She closed her eyes and felt James's breath stir the fine hairs at her temple and, when he bent to whisper to her, she felt the softness of his lips for an instant on her earlobe. But he said very little, and late in the evening she realized that he hadn't once implored her to speak.

He also hadn't told her that he loved her. She saw the flicker of worry in his eyes now and again, but more often she saw a distance growing in them, like he was far away and getting farther, following some dark trail of thoughts away from the circle of their tangent bodies.

A sick dread began to fill her. Perhaps, she worried, she'd waited too long. Perhaps her eccentricity had lost its charm and become merely inconvenient. Could it be that he was bored? Happiness can turn like a tide for a young girl in love, and Anamique's did. It turned and ebbed and left her leaden and miserable as she danced, and her misery only deepened when James didn't notice right away what she was sure was written on her face plain as words. Indeed, whole moments passed when he seemed entirely to forget her.

What, she wondered, could he be thinking about?

She lifted her hand from his arm and laid her fingertips gently against his cheek, startling him from his reverie. He looked down at her and saw at once the misery in her eyes. His face fell. 'Ana, please, don't look so sad,' he said. 'I'm a fool! I've the world's most beautiful girl in my arms and I let my thoughts get swept away with nonsense! You're all I want to think about.'

They were dancing past the verandah door and he swept her toward it and through it, out into the moonlight where they were alone. Truly alone, for the very first time.

James pushed the door closed, muffling the music and laughter within. And though they'd ceased dancing, he didn't drop his arm from her waist, but drew her nearer, her body full against his. He touched her lips with his fingertips, his brow furrowed and his eyes searching her face as if he were looking for the answer to some solemn mystery.

Anamique wanted to cry out, 'What's wrong?' but speech wouldn't come so easily. She asked him with her eyes.

In answer, James took something from his pocket. It was a little velvet box, and when he opened it, Anamique saw a small diamond on a thin gold band. She drew in her breath.

'Ana,' James whispered, 'will you marry me?'

She felt heat moving from her heart out through her limbs, and a flush spread up from the neckline of her gown, all the way over her shoulders and down to her fingertips. Her eyes filled with tears. All traces of misery were chased away by a flood of joy. She had dreamed of this moment so many times, and she had resolved what to do if it came. Reflexively, she bit her lip, but she released it again from between her teeth and hesitantly, wide-eyed and anxious, she opened her mouth to answer.

A look of panic flitted over James's face, and before Anamique could really register it, he leaned down fast and kissed her. He kissed her to stop her lips and in his urgency he wasn't tender about it. His teeth clashed against hers and her head knocked back against the wall. Her answer was lost in the jarring, and though her lips may have shaped the word 'yes,' she doubted James felt it, so hard was his mouth upon hers.

He drew slowly away and ventured a shame-faced look at her.

She was bewildered and breathless. That kiss, harsh with haste and teeth, it wasn't the kiss she had imagined in her daydreams. She'd never have dreamed James's lips could feel so *hard*. They may as well have been a hand clamped over her mouth.

She knew why. She looked up at him and spots of color flamed in her cheeks. He was afraid of her. After all of his cajoling and his scoffing at Providence, making her believe she could have a normal life, making her *dream* and *hope*, after all that, he was afraid of the curse!

She looked down at his hands. He had not yet slid the ring onto her finger but clutched at it. She took a step back.

'Ana—' James started to say, reaching for her, feebly holding out the ring. 'I'm sorry! I don't know what came over me. Please—'

She turned away, wiping her mouth with the back of her hand. Something was happening to her. Something was building in her, rising. Her breath came faster. Her skin felt feverish. Eighteen years of calm were swept away in a sudden wild rush, like the monsoon floods that ravage mangrove islands and whisk tigers out to sea. She wrenched open the door and ran inside, across the ballroom to the piano where she closed the keyboard so quickly the pianist had to snatch his fingers out. The dancers faltered in their fox-trot and turned to her, bright-eyed, breathless, and smiling. She saw her mother, her sisters. In the doorway, with anguish on his face, was James.

Anamique took a deep breath, parted her lips, and began to sing. It was Isolde that welled forth as her voice at last burst from its cage. It was the 'Liebestod,' and James's eyes filled with tears. Anamique's voice was wizardry. Honey. The others had just time to register the perfection of it with a kind of stunned euphoria before, as Anamique had really always believed it would, the curse came true.

· TEN ·

A Masterpiece

Anamique's powerful voice filled the house and even reached across the garden to the servants' quarters. Not a soul survived her soaring 'Liebestod.' Crouched in the garden, Vasudev heard the singing and as it entered his ears, he lapsed into a befuddled fugue. But he couldn't die of it – he hadn't been *alive* for centuries – and after the singing ceased, he blinked and shook off his confusion. An incredulous smile unfurled across his face and he gave a great whoop and a caper and he skittered back down to Hell to be there to count the souls as they drifted in.

There could be no doubt about it: This curse was his masterpiece!

On the rooftop where it had been spying, Pranjivan's shadow swayed mournfully on its kite string. It drifted down to the ground to peer in the window. It hadn't heard the singing, of course, as shadows have no ears, but it had seen a white-clad khitmutgar with a full tray of sherbet dishes suddenly freeze mid-stride and crumple to the ground, dead. And the khitmutgar wasn't the only one.

Inside the ballroom the British were very still. They had sunk to the floor, some still joined in the embrace of the dance, leaning together on their knees like marionettes at rest. Others had fallen over, and the ladies' ankles, protruding from their skirts, were very pale. A fly sauntered down the bridge of a nose. All their eyes were open.

There was a small movement in the doorway – Anamique's hand in James's hair as she cradled his head in her lap. She traced her fingertips over the planes of his face, across his jaw, feeling the roughness as she went against the grain. She touched the place where his dimples would be if he were to smile at her, which he wouldn't, she realized, ever again.

The whites of her eyes were wide rings around her irises, giving her the look of one startled from a nightmare. As Pranjivan's shadow watched, Anamique took a small ring from James's dead hands and slid it onto her finger, holding it up to the light so the tiny diamond sparkled.

Then she bent over him, pressed her face into the cooling flesh of his neck, and began to sob.

ELEVEN

The Beautiful Fire

Sixty-three,' Vasudev counted as the last of the partygoers and servants filed into the Fire. 'Sixty-three!' He skipped around the tea table, jubilant. It had taken eighteen years, but it had been worth the wait and worth the gamble. Such finery the British had worn to their deaths! Dinner jackets and gowns, and the ladies' lacy trims and feathers had sputtered such pretty sparks as the Fire drew them in.

The demon was desperate to gloat and he thought he would have to go back up into the world and dart past Pranjivan to dance around Estella's deathbed, but as it turned out, he didn't have to go anywhere. Estella came to him.

Vasudev saw her coming down the long onyx tunnel and the sight of her momentarily robbed him of words. She could no longer walk. With its kite string trailing behind it, Pranjivan's shadow carried her in its arms as easily and as gently as the old bitch herself had cradled the many infants' souls she had gleaned from the Fire in her long, strange career in Hell. She looked so fragile. The pins had fallen out of her hair and it hung loose and dragged across the floor like a long skein of spun silver. But for all her fragility and dishevelment, her eyes burned with their old fury.

Vasudev's moment of speechlessness passed and he crowed, 'My dear, how kind of you to come! Have you heard? Did you stop to see the bodies? Is it quite the talk of the town? Sixty-three! *Sixty-three.* I think we can all agree I win this round.'

Estella hissed, 'Vasudev, this cannot stand. It is out of all proportion!'

'Proportion? But what has proportion to do with anything? That's the beauty of spicy little curses such as these, Estella. You never know how they might play out. Don't get high and mighty now. You knew the rules!'

'Did Yama sanction your rules? Proportion is to be maintained. That is *his* rule.'

'You never cared about that rule when I let you have a few extra brats now and then, did you?' Vasudev sneered. 'You didn't mind a little curse so much then, when the lack of *proportion* was in your favor. You're just a sore loser.'

Estella started to respond but there was nothing to say. He was right. She had tolerated his perverse game of curses to serve her own ends, and this was the fruit of it: scores dead, and an innocent girl turned murderer of everyone she knew. In the shadow's arms, Estella's frail body sagged with defeat. There was nothing she could do. Saving these souls was beyond her. She had walked out of the Fire for the last time. When next that beautiful inferno enfolded her, it would be to cleanse her own sins and melt away her memories, and she wouldn't be coming back out until Yama set her soul in a new body, human or beast. That was how it worked. The Fire took in souls and made them new, and Yama sleeved them into new bodies as he saw fit. Estella might be reborn as a tigress or a river dolphin or an ibex that could balance on tiptoe on a mountaintop. Or she might be born as a woman again, perhaps one who could have love all her life instead of only the memory of it.

She found herself now staring at the flames with a look of longing.

She was ready; she had been ready for a long time. Her soul craved the Fire. Only one thing had kept her in this limbo of lingering death – a far worse death than she herself had ever inflicted on the wicked – and that was Vasudev. For sixty years, with the power Yama had given her, she had staved off the worst of the demon's bloodthirst, but she knew it had been building up in him and that it would find its terrible release the moment he was free of her.

'My dear,' he said now with exaggerated courtesy, 'you look very tired. Won't you sit?' He pulled a chair out for her at the tea table. 'Will you take some refreshment?' His lip pulled into a snarl. Unable to contain himself, he added, 'One last cup of tea before you burn, you old bitch?'

'No, thank you,' she replied. 'I've done playing at civility with you, demon.'

'Yes. *Done*. So you are! What are you waiting for? Go on. You can catch up to your countrymen if you hurry. Do you know what I am going to do the moment you're gone? "Pranjivan" might mean "life," but that won't protect him. Nothing will. I'm thinking up something slow for him, for all those years I had to knock on the tradesmen's door like some common peddler. And then? I've been saving this up, Estella. I'm going to go on a pilgrimage and seek out every brat you ever hauled back up to the world and make them wish they'd stayed dead the first time. Oh, I won't remember them all, but I'll do my best.'

Estella bade Pranjivan's shadow set her down and it did, though it stayed at her side and held her up as she took feeble steps toward Vasudev. Her voice was a rasp as she cried, 'Yama won't tolerate that, Vasudev. Do you hear me?'

'But how long will it take him to notice, do you think? When will he chance to visit our little neighborhood of Hell? When did he last?' He was taunting her. Estella sometimes imagined she felt the presence of the Lord of Hell passing close in the great Fire, but she had not seen or heard him for sixty years, since she first came here fresh with widow's grief and had this awful duty thrust upon her.

Now, her voice shaking, she whispered, 'You can't do this. . . .'

But Vasudev only laughed. 'Can't I? Go on and die, Estella. Our little arrangement couldn't last forever, and – my teeth! – it's lasted long enough. You never had any business here. Hell is no place for the living!'

At that moment they both heard an unmistakable sound in the corridor. Vasudev's eyes widened and Estella found the strength to stand straighter. It was footfall. In unison they turned to peer down the gleaming black tunnel. They both knew that souls drifted these byways as silently as butterflies. The dead made no sound of footfall.

Only the living did that.

Breathless, watching, they made out only a blur at first, and soon the shape of a girl, walking with a posture of rigid resolution such as one might bear when going to her doom. It was Anamique, her eyes still wide with shock. She held Pranjivan's kite string loosely in her fingers. She had followed it like a lifeline through the dark, and as she rounded the curve now and faced the Fire, she had to close her eyes against its brilliance.

When she opened them and blinked, she saw figures silhouetted against the Fire and went toward them. It had been months since she had glimpsed the old bitch in town and she was shocked by the change in her. Many times she had thought of knocking on the door of her palace or accosting her in the street, of testing the curse on the one who had delivered it. She had dreamed of it, but she never dared it. And now the old bitch stood before her as thin as the shaft of a feather and nearly translucent with frailty, and Anamique held her tongue. She wanted more than revenge. She wanted James back, and all the others, her parents and sisters, her ayah, and the old Rajput warrior who had swallowed his dignity to guide her pony around the yard. But if she spoke her questions aloud, she would only kill again and there would be no one left to tell her what to do.

'Have you come for him, child?' Estella asked.

Anamique nodded.

Vasudev chuffed. He had a sour, calculating look on his moon-round face. 'So sorry,' he said. 'Nothing to be done about it. The Lord of Hell will remake him, just like all the others. You're too late, you see.' He pointed to the Fire.

Anamique stared at it. Its glow lit her gray eyes orange and a look of despair came over her lovely face.

'Poor thing,' the demon said. 'Best just turn yourself around and get on out while you can.' He stepped forward and took Anamique's elbow in an almost kindly fashion, acting quite the small gentleman as he began to guide her back the way she'd come.

Dazed, the girl looked over her shoulder at Estella, who suddenly called out, 'Wait a moment, child.'

Vasudev grimaced. 'No time for nonsense, now. Come, come.'

Estella laughed once, sharply. 'What's the matter, Vasudev? Afraid of something?'

Vasudev scowled. 'Afraid? Bosh! Just concerned for the girl. This is no place for the living!'

'No, it isn't, is it?' Estella gave him a penetrating look. 'Anamique, come here,' she said.

Anamique went to her. Vasudev gritted his teeth. His eyes darted anxiously between the Fire and this living girl whose grief reminded him so much of Estella's grief, decades past.

Estella said, 'I regret that you were drawn into this demon's twisted world, dear girl. Your curse has been a lesion on my soul these eighteen years. You should know that because of it, twenty-two children survived an earthquake who would otherwise have died. Your curse saved all those lives. And these years of your silence, your strength has saved many more.'

'She didn't *save* anyone,' argued Vasudev peevishly. 'Choosing not to kill someone isn't the same as *saving* them.'

'A fine distinction, coming from you,' the old woman replied.

Anamique looked confused. Estella reached for her hand and clutched it. Her voice seemed to weaken now with every word she spoke. 'There's no cheating death,' she whispered. 'We will all pass through the purifying Fire and be reborn in the bodies we have earned, man or cricket, jackal or eagle. Those decisions are Yama's alone; my only influence has been *when*, and who deserved more time before the Fire. I have bought years for children, and there was no currency but trade. A dirty soul for a clean one, one to one, that's the way it works. But the day of your christening, Vasudev offered up twenty-two children for free. Of course they weren't really free.

Their price was the curse. It was a risk, and now it has proven a very bad bargain indeed.'

'This is all a fine education for the young lady, I'm sure,' Vasudev interrupted. 'But it's time she was getting out of here. Missy? Estella needs some peace so she can finally *die*.'

'Not quite yet,' Estella said, producing a flask from within the folds of her shawl and holding it out to Anamique. 'Child, quickly, drink this,' she said.

Vasudev gasped. 'No! You can't!' he sputtered.

Anamique looked back and forth between them, uncertain. Then Estella whispered, 'It's not too late to save him,' and Anamique took the flask and drank. It tasted of spice and herbs and burned going down and she felt it spreading through her in a way that made her aware of her moving blood and all its pathways.

Vasudev hopped around in an agitated dance, crying out, 'You can't! Yama will never sanction this!'

'A life for a life,' Estella said. 'That's how it works.' Ill as she was, skin taut over her fine bones, she still looked like some kind of goddess, the brilliant filaments of her hair riding the drafts of heat that pulsed through the passage. Her eyes were hard and clear and insistent. She repeated, 'A life for a life,' then added, 'Mine for his.'

Anamique stared at her. Pranjivan's shadow clung to its mistress. The demon growled, 'No! It won't do! Stop this nonsense at once!'

With grave intensity Estella looked into Anamique's eyes and said, 'Speak, child, and send my soul to the Fire. Follow, and I'll find your soldier for you. You can lead him out. Speak now,' she said urgently, pleading. 'Say anything. Say his name. *Please.*'

James, Anamique thought, holding his name on the tip of her tongue like the seed of an entire life that might, from that moment forward, grow entwined with her own like a lovely vine. But she couldn't say his name, not now. She wouldn't use it as a murder weapon. Estella's face was hopeful, pleading. Anamique wouldn't say James's name, but she had another idea. She exhaled slowly and then took a deep breath. And for the second time in her life, she let her voice out of its cage.

She sang.

When Estella heard her voice, in the moment just before her eyes rolled back in their sockets, she was transfigured by a look of joy. Then she collapsed. Pranjivan's shadow caught her and gathered her up.

Anamique had to blink. The shadow held the body in its arms, but Estella's soul still stood before her, weightless and joyous. Free. For a long moment she stood and listened as Anamique's voice soared, then she beckoned and turned and started toward the Fire on light, silent feet. She dove into the flames and the long tendrils of her gun-metal gray hair were the last to disappear. Gleaming like lit fuses, they wavered and snapped as the flames enfolded her completely.

Still singing, heart racing, Anamique followed.

Into the Fire.

It drew her in. It raged around her. She felt heat, but it didn't burn her. She felt as hard as a diamond. Distinct. She went on singing.

Behind her in the black tunnel, Vasudev was again stunned into a stupor by the sound of her voice. His eyes lost focus and his mouth fell slack, slaver stringing between his pointed teeth. Pranjivan's shadow still held Estella's frail old body in its arms. It glided slowly into the Fire behind Anamique, and unlike the stuff of souls, which may subsist within the inferno for ages untold, shadow and skin were of earthly make and were instantly incinerated, leaving nothing behind, not even ash.

In the Fire, Anamique's eyes were open and she saw countless souls drifting all around her, souls like alchemist's metal being transfigured in this great crucible, souls made molten, made new. She floated, following the tendrils of Estella's hair through the flames. She sang. With each and every note her soul knew a pang of joy, as if her voice escaped again and again from its accursed prison with every word.

And then, suddenly, she became aware of a presence nearby in the sea of flame, a magnificent and blistering intelligence hidden from view. It was Yama, Lord of Hell, and he was everywhere, invisible all around her, listening, and she went on singing every role she knew. Carmen, Manon, Euridice, Musetta, Isolde. The 'Liebestod', that lament for a dead love. She sang it all the way through this time.

And she was still singing when she found James spinning slowly in the flames. His eyes were open but unseeing. Her voice faltered to a stop.

'Exquisite,' said Yama.

Anamique looked around but saw no great shape or silhouette in the Fire. Perhaps, she thought, he *was* the Fire.

'Take your lover and go,' the Lord of Hell continued. 'And take the others too. Estella's soul shall suffice in trade for them all. But there is an additional price.'

'I will pay any price,' Anamique said. These were the first words she had ever spoken that came not from an opera libretto but from her own heart, and she meant them. *Any price.*

'You will serve in her place as Ambassador to Hell.'

Anamique felt a spasm of fear but she nodded. 'Anything,' she repeated. The heat was rising. She began to feel the muted movement of the flames against her flesh as the tonic lost its potency. At that moment she was shunted backward very quickly, tumbling head over heels until she was thrown clear of the Fire. She fell and felt the hot onyx floor against her face. She rose to her feet, saw Vasudev standing by the tea table, coming out of his trance. She didn't see James or the others and she didn't turn round to look for them. She began again to sing, and she picked up the scorched end of Pranjivan's kite string and followed it out of Hell. She had learned from Orpheus's mistake, and did not look back.

· T W E L V E ·

The Ambassador to Hell

James's wife never told him that she loved him, not out loud, but he learned to believe it anyway. There are other ways of showing someone you love them, such as fetching them out of Hell. Their wedding was small, just the two of them with Pranjivan – eternally shadowless now – and Anamique's parents and sisters, who recalled every moment of their strange resurrections. They all stood with the minister in the garden, and Anamique mouthed the words of her vows in silence while James spoke softly, his voice husky and tremulous with emotion.

After, there was a wide white bed with a cocoon of mosquito netting stirred by a punkah fan, and cool limbs entwined beneath a white sheet. This time when Anamique and James kissed, there was no dread or haste or clash of teeth, but only lingering and sweetness, and lips straying from lips to taste the curves of each other's throats and shoulders, the palms of hands, the fluttering fragility of eyelids, the smooth, arched valleys of backs. The silent bride bit down on her lip so nothing could coax a killing sound from her, not pleasure and not pain, and she discovered both without a murmur.

As the years went by, a cradle was thrice filled and Anamique bit down on a leather strap for each birth: two boys, then a girl. The boys were born without so much as a moan from their beautiful mother, but the girl, a wily stargazer, drove a single cry from her and she had to stagger down the onyx passage, wild-eyed and wrapped in the blood-stained sheet of her childbed, to win back her baby from the Fire. Vasudev cowered behind the tea table and made no attempt to barter with her, and once her tiny girl's soul was cradled safe in her arms, Anamique sang her a lullaby. It was the only lullaby she would ever sing, and it was sung in Hell.

Unlike her family, Vasudev heard Anamique's voice often and it had the same hypnotic effect each time. He found, to his everlasting bitterness, that his spicy little curse had had an unintended consequence: It gave this new Ambassador a power her predecessor had never ever dreamed of. All she had to do was sing and Vasudev was lost. The music flowed into him like a river and swept all his malice away, and when he awakened from his trance, he would hear himself muttering preposterous things like, 'Whatever you think best,' or, 'Of course, my dear, *all* the children shall survive the flood.'

During Anamique's tenure in Hell, he ground his teeth down to stubs in his frustration, but he still appeared each morning like clockwork at the little table, carrying a fresh pot of tea and a flask of tonic. He still dreamed up curses to inflict upon humanity, but they fluttered right out of his mind the moment Anamique released her voice from its cage. Though she herself had always thought of it as a songbird, to Vasudev it was a bird of prey, devouring his will, and the worst of it was the knowledge that he himself had dreamed up its awful power.

Yama often hovered near to hear Anamique sing, and she brought down new songs for as long as she lived. For decades this particular byway of Hell rang with music, and in that time many children lived, their souls returned gladly in trade for those of ruthless men and joyless, grasping women, slave traffickers and opium dealers, sepoy traitors and brutal tribesmen, corrupt nawabs and great white hunters, and every other species of villain that made its way onto Pranjivan's list.

The wicked in this part of the world endured rueful decades of early death, and the Fire burned hot and bright and remade them all, and they were all in their turn born back into the world as carp and macaques and salamanders and mosquitoes with no recollection of their human lives or the Fire that followed, but only faint memories of music, like wisps of a dream, from their last glimmering moments in Hell.

· HATCHLING ·

· HATCHLING ·

Six days before Esmé's fourteenth birthday, her left eye turned from brown to blue. It happened in the night. She went to sleep with brown eyes, and when she woke at dawn to the howling of wolves, her left eye was *blue*. She had just slipped out of bed when she noticed it. She was headed to the window to look for the wolves – wolves in London, of all impossible things! But she didn't make it to the window. Her eye flashed at her in the mirror, pale as the wink of a ghost, and she forgot all about the wolves and just stared at herself.

It was no trick of the light. Her eye was an eerie white-blue, the color of ancient ice in a place that never thaws, and as startling as it was, there was something profoundly familiar about it too. Esmé's blood quickened as a shock of memories pulsed through her: a world of snow and spires; a milky mirror framed in jewels; the touch of warm lips on hers.

Esmé swayed on her feet. These weren't her memories. This wasn't her eye. She clamped a hand over it and ran to wake her mother.

Esmé climbed up onto her mother's high bed and perched beside her on her knees. Mab's hair was woven into a single long braid and coiled around her neck like a pet serpent, and she was asleep, her white eyelids fluttering in some deep dream. Esmé reached for her shoulder but hesitated. She hated to wake her mother if she wasn't having one of her nightmares – Mab was plagued by nightmares and found little enough rest in sleep. So many nights, so many mornings, she woke screaming and Esmé soothed her as if she were the mother and Mab the child.

Indeed, now that Esmé was nearly grown, it was hard to tell them apart at a glance. They were so alike, and Mab was so young. They were both small and beautiful with long, long hair as red as persimmons. They laughed alike and moved alike, and they thought the same thoughts as completely as if a butterfly traveled back and forth between their minds, bearing ideas on its legs like pollen. But they didn't share nightmares. Esmé didn't know what her mother dreamed about. Mab would never tell, just as she would never talk about her life before Esmé was born.

She said only that she was an orphan. Esmé didn't even know what language her mother had spoken before, just that she had learned English when Esmé was a baby. Mab's accent was like spice, and out at the shops and the theaters, whenever she had to speak to men, they seemed to Esmé to want to taste the words right off her mother's lips. The way they looked at her! But the way Mab looked back could freeze the saliva in their mouths. There was no room in her life for men, or for anyone but Esmé. It was just the two of them. It always had been.

Softly Esmé touched her mother's shoulder and whispered, 'Mama . . .'

Mab woke with a gasp and came upright, wild-eyed, in an instant.

'It's just me,' said Esmé gently.

'Esmé,' said Mab, collapsing back into her pillows. 'I . . . I was dreaming.'

'I know, Mama.'

'Is it late? Have I slept late?'

'No, it's only dawn.'

'Oh. What is it, darling?' Mab murmured. 'Is something the matter?'

In a small voice, Esmé said, 'It's my eye, Mama. Something's the matter with my eye.'

Mab drew herself up on one elbow and turned Esmé toward the window to see her better. She was smiling sleepily and her fingers were gentle on Esmé's cheek, but when the dull light glittered over the blue of her daughter's eye, she recoiled in horror and let out a strangled cry. *'Ayaozhdya!'* The word flew from her lips and her lovely face twisted into a snarl.

Esmé reeled back, shocked. She tumbled off the high bed and plunged down to the floor, landing hard on her elbow. Mab leapt down beside her and Esmé felt the sting of her mother's braid as it snapped at her cheek like a whip. 'Mama!' she cried, flinching away.

Her mother caught her by the shoulders, her nails cutting into Esmé's skin like talons. White-faced and ferocious, she stared into Esmé's blue eye and hissed in a jagged language that seemed made for cursing. *'Druj dregvantem! Thaeshavant en uthem ni!'* She spat the words out like poison and Esmé could only wilt in her grasp, stunned to see her mother so transformed.

'What's wrong?' she gasped.

'Druj ayaozhdya!' Mab cried. Esmé tried to turn her head aside but her mother grabbed her chin and held her fast. Her face was so close to Esmé's face. Her own brown eyes appeared entirely black from her enlarged pupils as she stared into Esmé's blue eye and, with a guttural sob, broke into English. 'Beast bastards! Get out of her!'

Esmé began to sob too. She pleaded, 'Mama! Wake up, please!' thinking her mother must still be mired in her nightmares. 'It's *me*!' She said it again and again. 'It's me. It's *me*!'

Mab blinked. She stared at Esmé. She was still wild-eyed but the savagery slowly left her face and her fingers loosened on Esmé's shoulder and chin. Her chest heaving, she whispered thickly, 'Esmé? Is it really only you? Are you certain?'

Esmé nodded, sobbing raggedly, and for a few moments they stared at each other like strangers. Then Mab wrapped her arms around her daughter and held her close, rocking her and whispering, 'I'm so sorry, my darling. I'm so sorry I frightened you,' and they both wept until their breathing calmed.

'What is it, Mama?' Esmé whispered. 'What did I do?'

'You didn't do anything, darling. It wasn't you I was talking to.'

'Then . . . *who*?' Esmé sat back and looked at her mother.

Seeing the blue eye again, Mab shuddered and whispered, '*Avo afritim*. Bless and protect us.' Her face and lips were white and bloodless as paper as she told Esmé, 'Cover your eye, darling. They might be . . . *using* it.'

Esmé put her hand up over her eye and said, '*Using* it?'

'Has someone spoken to you, Esmé? Has someone stared into your eyes and made you stare back?'

'What?' asked Esmé. She was rarely out of her mother's company to meet strangers. 'No.'

'Have you seen any one-eyed birds?'

'One-eyed birds?' Esmé repeated. With a sick feeling she remembered a trip to the seaside when she was a little girl, how her mother had kicked and shrieked at a one-eyed seagull like a madwoman and chased it away, then clutched Esmé tight like a doll all the way back to London on the train.

'One-eyed anything. Crows, pigeons, cats,' Mab persisted.

Esmé shook her head again.

'Has *anything* happened, anything strange?'

'Strange?' Esmé asked, an unaccustomed edge of bitterness to her voice. 'Our whole life is strange!'

She hadn't even realized it for so long, how small and unreal their life was, just the two of them in a world of their own creation. All around them roared a great city, a tumult of engines and voices, yet they knew no one. They had no friends and no family and never even answered the door when neighbors knocked.

But if they knew no one, somewhere out there in that seething world of folk, someone knew *them*, because someone sent them diamonds. They arrived by post, loose in plain airmail envelopes with no return address. Mab kept them in a saltshaker and every few weeks they took the Tube to Hatton Garden, knocked on the back door of a jeweler's shop, and sold one or two to a fat woman with a mouth like a prune. They called these trips their 'diamond days,' and went afterward to small, neat shops to buy artichokes and cherries and pink boxes of baklava, books and sheet music, pearl buttons and embroidery thread and lengths of antique lace.

Everything was strange and nothing was! Was it strange that Esmé had never been to school, or to a hairdresser, or even to a doctor? It was Mab who had taught her to read and count and play the violin, and Mab who trimmed her hair, and as for the doctor, neither of them had ever fallen ill. They drank a daily dose of tea that Mab mixed from herbs, and that was the extent of their medicine. A few months ago when Esmé's bleeding had first come, her mother had turned pale and wept, so Esmé thought for a panicked moment that she must be dying, but Mab had explained in a rush that it meant she wasn't a child anymore. That she could breed. She'd made it sound like something animals did – *breed* – and she'd had such terrible nightmares that night she'd awakened the whole building with her screams.

It was also on that night, when her mother's screams woke her, that Esmé thought she glimpsed a man standing on the church steeple across the street, staring in her window. But when she looked again, her heart giving a great lurch, there hadn't been anyone there.

That day and night, the bleeding and the screaming, had knocked something askew for Esmé, like a picture swinging crooked on a wall. She loved the life she lived with her mother. It was beautiful. It was, she sometimes thought, a sweet emulation of the fairy tales they cherished in their lovely, gold-edged books. They sewed their own clothes from bolts of velvet and silk, ate all their meals as picnics, indoors or out, and danced on the rooftop, cutting passage-ways through the fog with their bodies. They embroidered tapestries of their own design, wove endless melodies on their violins, charted the course of the moon each month, and went to the theater and the ballet as often as they liked – every night last week to see *Swan Lake* again and again. Esmé herself could dance like a faerie, climb trees like a squirrel, and sit so still in the park that birds would come to perch on her. Her mother had taught her all that, and for years it had been enough. But she wasn't a little girl anymore, and she had begun to catch hints and glints of another world outside her pretty little life, one filled with spice and poetry and strangers.

Twice now the boy from the flower shop had smiled at her, his whole face flushing pink as he did, and when he was behind her in line at the bakery last week, he'd held her long braid gently in his hand, thinking she wouldn't feel it, but she had. She hadn't turned around, but she'd blushed and stammered ordering her cakes, and she'd left in a rush, imagining she could feel his touch all the way up her braid and tingling at the nape of her neck. She didn't even know his name. She didn't know anyone's name.

'What's wrong with us?' she demanded now. 'Why are we such freaks? Why don't we have any friends? Why don't we have any family?'

'I know our life is . . . *different*. I just . . .' Mab faltered. 'Darling, I just didn't know how to do it. I did the best I could!'

'What do you mean?' Esmé cried in frustration, as for the first time her confusion broke out of her and overwhelmed her calm, quiet nature. 'You didn't know how to do what? *Live?*'

'No! I didn't! I had to learn it all, Esmé, after you were born. How to cross a street and turn on a faucet and light a match? How to tie shoes? Use money?' She took a deep, uneven breath, hesitated, and then said quietly, 'And I had to learn how to look at someone without being afraid they would come in through my eyes and wear my skin like a costume while I was shoved into the shadows of my own soul!' Her voice quavered and rose with a hint of hysteria. Esmé stared at her, baffled by her words, and she knew that whatever had happened, whatever was happening, the pretty little life she had always known was coming to a close. Something new was beginning.

'What are you talking about, Mama?' she asked, more gently. She was on her knees, with her hair falling loose around her and radiating out across the floor, as red in the dawn light as a spill of blood. In her white nightgown she looked very young and very fragile, and Mab reached out a shaking hand and clasped her daughter's fingers.

'Esmé, you haven't seen any . . .' she began uneasily but her voice gave out and she swallowed and started again. 'You haven't seen or heard any . . . *wolves*, have you?'

And Esmé remembered in a rush – the wolfsong, the haunting, lyrical spirals of it in the dawn quiet and the feeling of euphoria that had attended it. Even in recollection the howling uplifted her like the crescendo at the end of a symphony and made her heartbeat quicken. Eyes wide, she nodded. 'This morning,' she said. 'That's what woke me.'

Mab's eyelids fluttered like she might faint. She steadied herself with one hand splayed upon the floor and gasped for breath. 'No, oh no,' she said very faintly. 'They've found us.' She rose suddenly, went to the window, and scanned the street below before winching the curtains closed.

'Who's found us, Mama?' asked Esmé.

Mab turned to her. 'I didn't want their ugliness in your mind, my darling. That's why I never told you about them, about my life before—'

'You mean the people who raised you?'

'They aren't *people!*' Mab snapped. 'They can hear the blood moving in your veins a mile away. They can smell the color of your hair in the dark. They're hunters, Esmé, and they never grow old, they never die, and they can't *love*. They're empty, and they're vicious, and I . . . I *stole* you from them!' Her hands went to her slim stomach, cupping it as if her arms were remembering a time when it had been round and full. Her voice dropped to a whisper. 'Fourteen years ago I escaped from them with you like a treasure inside of me. I used to be so afraid they'd find us, but I . . . I'd started to believe we were safe.'

'You . . . you think they've found us now?'

'The Druj take many shapes, but the hunters are always wolves. And their eyes . . . their eyes are always blue. Pale, pale blue. Like yours.'

Stunned by all she was hearing, Esmé let her hand drop from her eye. Mab cringed at the sight of it. *'Druj daevas!'* she hissed. 'Cover that up, Esmé! I can't stand the sight of it! It's just like *hers*.'

'Whose?'

'Never mind. We have to leave. But first, bring me some scissors.'

'Why?' Esmé asked with a quaver in her voice, her hand pressing protectively against her eye.

'Just bring them, darling.'

Trembling, Esmé did as she was told.

Ten minutes later they went down the fire escape and left their small, sweet world behind. Esmé wore an eye patch hastily cut from the velvet bedspread, and they both carried violin cases filled with such essentials as nightgowns and passports and their saltshaker full of diamonds. Everything else they left behind, their fairy tale books and their dresses and violins, and, dangling from the chandelier, they left two long, long, red, red braids. Crossing the street, they looked like musicians hurrying to rehearsal, swinging their violin cases.

Esmé kept reaching up to touch her head. She felt so light without her hair, like she might float up into the sky, but Mab grabbed her hand and held it tight, and Esmé knew she'd never let her drift away.

· T W O ·

Fangs and Love

The howls of the hunt had died away with the dawn, so Mihai relaxed his surveillance of Esmé's window. He was stiff from crouching atop the church steeple all night; such a job as this was better performed as a crow, but he didn't shift shape anymore – not even to wolf shape, however much his body craved the change. He lived each moment in human cithra, comfortable or not. It was who he was now. It had its limitations, but it had its benefits too. He was certain the Tajbel wolves, snuffling now into whatever dark place they had found to pass the daylight hours, would agree.

He smiled grimly. They'd caught his scent last night and circled the church baying, but they couldn't scale the walls and get him, not as they were, and anyway, it wasn't him they'd come for, but Esmé. Even so, he thought, they'd be happy to tear off his head for what he'd done to them fourteen years ago. The Druj taboo against killing their own did not apply to exiles, and it certainly didn't apply to traitors.

He saw Esmé's small shape hurry past her window and he thought of gliding right across the street to her fire escape, but he hesitated. All these years, and the time had finally come. There were actually butterflies in his stomach! He could have laughed at himself – a Druj hunter, nervous, and not because the wolves had finally found him, but because of this one small girl!

He would have to get her away before nightfall, before the wolves came out again. It was just past dawn now. He had time. He decided to go for a cup of tea first and settle his nerves.

Thinking the church courtyard below was deserted, he climbed down the tower headfirst like a lizard, but some nuns were coming out through an archway and gasped at the sight of him. They crossed themselves and stumbled back in panic – all but one of them. One steely-eyed crone marched right up to him as he leapt to the ground. 'Druj devil!' she spat. 'Leave this holy place!' And she took a pinch of ash from a pouch and flung it in his face.

Mihai coughed, surprised to find a city nun armed against the Druj. City humans almost never recognized his kind or knew how to protect against them. She must be from the mountains, he thought, from far away to the south and east where a human's life could depend upon a firebrand and a pouch of ash. He brushed the grit from his eyelashes, gave her a polite bow, and went on his way. She stood rooted in place and watched him go. She was flummoxed, and he knew why. The ashes had stung, but they should have burned him, sure as acid. Once, they would have, just as they would any Druj. Once, Mihai had been like the others, but not anymore.

The girl in the tea shop flushed when she saw him, and he knew she'd been watching for him. 'Good morning, blossom,' he said in his soft voice, smiling just enough to show his sharp canines. In the cheerful light of the shop he looked feral and deadly. The fangs, his stature, his long black hair, and his eyes, pale as a Siberian husky's against his black lashes and brows, made Mihai hard not to notice, and hard not to think about after.

'Good morning, you,' the girl said, blushing from her bright blue hair to her throat and down into the shadow of her blouse. Following the blush down, Mihai could see the small ink spike of a tattoo emerging from the cleft between her breasts. It looked like it might be the point of a star. 'Did you hear the wolves?' she asked him.

He lifted his gaze and raised his eyebrows, feigning surprise. 'Wolves?'

'Just before dawn,' she said. She was pretty. Her eyes were large and bright, just the kind that had always called to him, and Mihai found himself thinking from old habit that she'd be so easy to slip into. He shook off the idea. 'We all heard them howling,' she told him. 'It was mad.'

'Wolves in the city?' He gave her a skeptical look. 'That *is* mad. Maybe it was all a dream.'

'No. I even heard about it on the radio,' she insisted. 'They're saying they must have escaped from some wildlife smugglers or something.'

'I'll have to keep an ear out,' he said.

'Some of us are going up to the roof tonight to watch for them,' she said, adding shyly, 'You could come.'

Mihai only smiled at her, and he saw how her gaze lingered on his fangs.

She gave him his tea for free, slipping chocolates onto the dish and brushing her knuckles across his as she handed it to him. Her face was luminous and hopeful; she'd go into the dark with him in a heartbeat, sharp teeth and all. Human girls were stupid that way. No, not stupid. Primal in their skin, without even knowing it. The things that made their pulse quicken were all the wrong things, but Mihai didn't take advantage of it, except for the free tea. He'd been waiting fourteen years for someone else, all fever and slick teeth and longing, and judging by the furor of the wolves last night, he didn't have much longer to wait. For Druj to hunt openly in a human city, so far from their dominion in remote mountains, they had to be crazed with a long-sought scent.

It was almost time. Esmé was nearly ripe.

While Mihai sipped his tea, he found himself so anxious he could hardly sit still. He thumbed idly through a free newspaper, the kind with music reviews and advice for lovers. He enjoyed human music as he enjoyed their tea: casually. It was their plain discussions of *love* that enthralled him. As if it were no more a mystery than bread or arithmetic! As if it were not utterly unique to them in the catalog of all things that had ever lived, on all planes, in all of time. Love was theirs alone, and it was why Mihai had helped a red-haired girl escape from Tajbel fourteen years ago with her belly full of child, and why he waited alone in this gray city, year after year, his mind on fire with hope.

Fourteen years, and his waiting was over.

Mihai winked at the blue-haired girl and left the tea shop, seeing wistfulness in her eyes as he turned away. He cut across the street with his head tilted back, his predator's senses filtering through the hundreds of fresh human trails until he picked out Mab's and Esmé's. In his mind their scent was the color of their hair, and it grew brighter as he drew nearer to their flat. He followed it up the fire escape to their ash-dusted window ledge and peered in. Their fragrance was bright and coppery – he could almost *taste* them – but the flat was quiet, no stir of breath or murmur of moving blood.

Then he saw the braids hanging from the chandelier, and he knew that they'd fled. He felt an instant flood of fury at Mab's trickery, and a twinge of panic to think of them getting away, but those feelings were quickly drowned out by the visceral thrill that came over him – despite everything he wanted to be, and all he tried to *un*-be – at the thought of a hunt.

THREE

Black Meadows

Some say the Druj are demons, children of chaos brought forth long ago to plague the archangels and seed wickedness into human hearts. Others call them *fey*, forest spirits who hunt hunters, born of the bones of the earth before mountains were mountains or God was God. Most people have never heard of them at all, and of those who have, many are inclined to believe they're just folk tales and fancy. But there are yet good people in this world who know too well that they're real. Who have been pierced by them, like an icicle through the soul, haunted by them, and hunted by them, and whose nightmares won't let them forget it.

There are places in the furls and fissures of mountains, from the Zagros to the Tien Shan and even as far west as the Carpathians, where humans never stray into the forests, not to hunt or gather firewood, not to meet secret lovers, and not to hide. They go no farther than the edges of the black meadows, those ashen strips they burn to divide their land from the forests.

Twice yearly, on the equinoxes, village elders tend to the meadows. It is only the hunched and white-haired who will go so near the forests, and for good reason: Druj aren't tempted by the old. So while the young wait in the safety of the villages, the old go forth and scorch the boundary meadows with firebrands. After the black grass cools, they walk across it, feeling it crunch and crackle under their soles, and they leave their tithes just under the forest's first shadows for the Druj to come and carry away. Brandy, bread, dried fruit and meat, sugar, knives, baskets of new kittens with their eyes still tight. Tales tell that the Druj don't eat, so the humans don't know who the food is for and they don't ask. They simply do as their own grandparents taught them, leave the baskets and keep their eyes down, no matter how great the temptation to peer into the forest. They don't want to see what might peer back.

The forests belong to the Druj. Everything in them belongs to the Druj and the Druj are supposed to stay there – agreements had been made – but sometimes boredom gets the better of them.

Boredom is a terrible affliction of the soulless.

Every village in the foothills of those varied mountains has its tales of Druj stalking among them. They come as crows and owls, foxes and magpies, stags whose antlers carry the moss of centuries, and wolves, huge and hunched, padding silently through the center of town. Whatever cithra they keep, their eyes are always the same, that desolate blue, and that's how humans know them. When they come as animals, they perch on rooftops or at the market's edge and watch in their terrible unblinking way, and the villagers go inside and bar their doors to wait until they leave. They might fright a young girl or boy by following them home, but usually in animal cithra they don't do much more than that.

When they come for mischief, they come as humans.

The story is nearly always the same, and it might go something like this:

'The youngest Margitay girl, the pretty one, she heard her cat mewling piteous by the sheds so she took her lantern out after him, and that cat's cries got farther off whilst she followed, till she found she was under the big black poplar in the bottom of the field. There in the darkness like a shadow's own shadow stood a stranger. He was mewling to sound just like her cat, but he stopped when she came near and he smiled to bare his fangs. He was beautiful as the devil's reflection and she couldn't help but stare at him, black-haired and sharp-toothed, with those eyes that shone like coins in a frozen wishing well. She knew what he was and she knew she should run, but like she'd grown roots she stood there whilst he came to her, and she never even moved when he slid his long, cold fingers under her chin and tipped her face up to his, like he might give her a kiss.

'But it wasn't a kiss he gave her. He fixed her brown eyes with his blue ones, and she knew she should squeeze hers shut. She'd been taught since she was a suckling that there are a hundred things the Druj can do with eyes! They can fish out your soul and keep it for a trophy, or they can pass visions in and plant dreams that will grow in the dark like toadstools. They can pluck out your eyeballs and put them in their pockets, or they can whisper spells that will turn your glance into a curse to wither crops and cripple horses!

'Or they can use your eyes as windows and climb inside you, shoving their dark animus into your soul and filling it, like brutal fingers thrust into a child's glove.

'That's what the stranger did to the pretty Margitay daughter. When he looked into her eyes, she felt a rush of cold fill her, like frigid water from a pump, and then everything fell into shadow. It was morning before she knew herself again. Birds were twittering and she was sagging on her feet, still standing under that black poplar. But there was no stranger before her, only her cat up in the branches. She wanted to think it had all been a dream, but there were leaves in her hair and a hollow ache through and through her, and she knew the demon had not left her pristine as he'd found her. Memories of the dark hours rose in waves to engulf her and she just dropped to her knees there and moaned.'

There are other, more savage versions of the same simple story, and they are never told full-voice like a fireside tale, but only in rough whispers beside children's beds to scare the fear of the night into them, and rightly so.

Druj *wear* humans. They aren't supposed to do it but they do, and they wear them harshly, for fighting and rutting and dancing and other such things as make mortal blood flow fast. And when they're through with them, they leave them where they found them, flow back into their own cold bodies, and return to the forest. The humans live. Over time their torn and bruised souls regain some semblance of their former shape. They live, but they are ever afterward tormented by nightmares.

Wolves

Esmé fiddled with her eye patch, wondering if the world would look different through her blue eye than it did through her brown one. When she thought her mother wasn't looking, she lifted the velvet a little and peered around the train car. Everything looked the same.

'Esmé!' Mab scolded. 'Leave that alone.'

Esmé quickly set the patch back in place. 'But people will think something's wrong with my eye,' she said. Already the handsome waiter in the dining car had given her a curious look.

'Something *is* wrong with your eye,' Mab reminded her.

'I mean, they'll think it's gross. Or *missing*. But it's kind of pretty, like one of those dogs, you know, the ones that catch Frisbees?' Mab only looked at her, nonplussed, and after a moment Esmé added, 'Isn't it bad enough I look like a boy with my hair cut off? I have to look like a *pirate* boy?'

'You do not look like a boy,' said Mab distractedly.

'So I do look like a pirate?'

Mab sighed. 'Leave the eye patch on, darling. Please.'

Shorn hair or not, Esmé did *not* look like a boy, and Mab certainly didn't either. When they had hurried to the train station with their violin cases, they had drawn almost as many stares as they would on any normal day when their hair was to their knees and sheeting behind them like red silk. A poetic fruit-seller had told them once that they looked like dryads, and they did still, only now they looked like dryads who had tired of snagging their hair on brambles and sliced it all off on the edge of a knife.

'What have they done to me, Mama?' Esmé asked now. 'Is it what they did to you?'

'No,' Mab said, and the word came out hard as fingers snapping. Esmé blinked at her mother, surprised. She was usually so patient, her voice so soft. 'This is *not* what they did to me,' Mab said. 'I haven't seen it before. When the Queen would . . . go inside of me . . . she liked to look in her mirror through my eyes as if . . . as if *she* was *me*, so I know my eyes didn't change color, and neither did *his*. . . .' she trailed off, looking down.

'What?' Esmé asked. 'Who?'

But Mab didn't say. She pressed her lips together for a moment and then went on. 'Their spies don't have eyes like that either. They have only one eye and the Queen keeps the other in her tabernacle. Only Druj have those eyes.'

'But I'm not one of them!' Esmé said. She was suddenly electrified by a horrifying thought. She had never asked about her father. She had never really asked about any of it. She realized now that she'd been afraid to learn what lay coiled at the roots of her mother's nightmares. She hadn't wanted any part of a history that could make someone scream like that. But she *was* part of it. She had come out of it, somehow. She asked, 'My . . . my father wasn't one of *them*, was he?'

Mab shuddered. 'No, darling, no. The Druj don't breed.'

'Oh,' said Esmé, relieved. 'Then, who *was* my father?'

Her mother hesitated before saying slowly, 'He was a boy, as I was a girl, not much older than you are now. The Queen chose him for me for the color of his hair.'

'What color was it?'

'The same as mine, exactly, and the same as yours. It took her months to find him and bring him back on her sledge. I didn't know anything about the world then, what lay beyond the forest, but now I know he was Russian. His name was Arkady.' She had a faraway look in her eyes, remembering.

Esmé asked, 'Was he nice?'

'Nice?' Mab gave a soft laugh. 'Not at first. He hated me like he hated them. He didn't understand what I was; I didn't either. He was the first human I'd ever seen. The first time I touched him and felt that his flesh was warm like mine, not cold like theirs, I can't explain it, my darling, that was the first time I understood I was *real*. He wasn't nice at first, but why should he have been? They had stolen him! But in time, between us, there was tenderness.'

Esmé was silent for a moment, staring at her mother. There was so much she didn't understand that she didn't even know where to begin asking. 'Mama, what do you mean, what you *were*? What *were* you?'

But Mab shook her head and looked out the window. 'Enough talking about them, darling. Please.'

'But what about my father? Arkady. What happened to him?'

Still looking out the window, Mab whispered, 'I don't know. I don't know what they did with him, after.'

The word 'after' hung heavy between them and Esmé wished she hadn't asked. That simple word managed to conjure a whole universe of unspeakable possibilities. 'Maybe he got away,' she said. '*You* got away.'

'Yes, but I couldn't have done it alone. I had help.'

'From who?'

'One of them. He was a Naxturu – that's what the wolves are called. Nocturnal, it means. They're the highest caste of Druj.'

'Why did he help you?'

'*Us*, darling. He helped *us*, and I never knew why. Now eat your soup. We've a long way to go. You'll need your strength.'

Esmé frowned. 'What about you? You haven't eaten any.'

Mab had just been stirring her soup in circles. Now she lifted her spoon and took a tiny sip from it. 'There,' she said. And slowly, in silence, they ate their soup without tasting a thing.

'Mama,' said Esmé after the handsome waiter had cleared away their bowls. 'Don't you think the wolves can follow us through the train tunnel?'

'We should have some time,' answered Mab. 'They only hunt at night. They draw power from the moon and they're strongest when it's nearest.'

'But it's not near now,' said Esmé. 'It's almost in apogee.' She'd been charting the monthly moons with her mother her whole life, and she finally knew why.

'That's good for us,' said Mab. 'They won't be at full strength.'

Esmé knew somehow that it wouldn't matter, that they would be strong enough. She could almost see them lunging out of the darkness, slaver clinging to their yellow fangs. She also knew, somehow, that they wouldn't stop until they found her, and she wondered why she wasn't more afraid. 'What do they want?' she asked in a hushed voice.

Mab only smiled at her and reached for her hand. If she knew what they wanted – and by the fear in her eyes Esmé could tell that she did – she wasn't going to tell.

The train sped on, out of its undersea tunnel and onto the plains of France. By and by they arrived in Paris and transferred to a train bound for Marseilles, where Mab planned to get them on a ship for Africa or the Canary Islands, or perhaps a boat that would never again come to a shore but just sail and sail where the wolves would never find them. But when they reached the port in Marseilles, they learned the next passenger ship wouldn't depart until morning. It was bound for Tunis and would leave at dawn.

Night was falling.

Mab knew that back in London the hunters would be waking up in whatever dark place they had used for a lair. They had probably slept in their human cithrim as they usually had back in Tajbel. Erezav and Isvant would be among them, the Queen's favorites who looked like beasts no matter what cithra they kept, wolf or man or even crow. They made vicious crows, and picked out humans' eyes just for looking at them. And the Queen herself, she would be there too, not as a wolf but as a woman. She might be riding one of her wolves, her long fingers clutching the fur of its nape. Mab shuddered at the vision of the Queen astride one of her massive black beasts. She knew the hunters couldn't reach Marseilles for hours, but the sight of the rising moon still sent a thrill of panic through her. 'Come on,' she said, grabbing Esmé by the hand.

They found a hotel and took a room high in the attic. It had a round window that looked out over the harbor, and it had one big bed. Mab and Esmé huddled in it. They burned the pages of a romance novel someone had left behind and spread the ashes around the bed, keeping some in their fists and the laps of their nightgowns, ready to throw. 'Ashes burn them,' Mab told Esmé.

'Why?' asked Esmé, looking at her dirty fingers. She found the sensation of the ashes unpleasant.

'I don't know. They abhor fire. I never knew of fire until I left them.'

They fell silent for a long time, listening.

Esmé slept and she dreamed of a moon framed by a rough rock window, and of a bed of furs, and of silver eyelids winking open on hinges to disclose real eyes, bloodshot and sticky. She dreamed of the pressure of warm lips against hers and she tasted river water on them and saw snowflakes caught in long, dark hair. She woke and listened in the dark for the howl of wolves but she heard only city sounds.

Mab had stayed awake all night and her eyes were glassy with exhaustion. 'It's time to go,' she said.

It was dawn. The tattered lace of darkness still hung over the city, as if night were a grim bride trudging to the horizon, trailing her shadowy train. They hurried the short blocks to the waterfront and merged there into a sleepy knot of passengers waiting to board a ship. The minutes dragged past and with each the glow of morning crept a little farther up the sky, until Mab and Esmé began to believe they would escape.

The first howl, when it came, was very far away, an eerie wisp of sound that might have been something else: a siren, or a grief-stricken woman. But Mab and Esmé both knew it wasn't something else. They felt it in their spines and in their souls. They spun, listening, staring, searching. The next howl was closer, and the next closer still. 'Mama, they're coming!' Esmé cried, and Mab heard excitement in her voice and saw that her face was vivid with it.

'Esmé!' she said sharply, and grabbed her hand. The passengers were lumbering across a narrow gangway onto the ship, and she shoved past them, dragging Esmé behind her. Lazy curses followed them as Mab thrust their tickets into the porter's hand and hurried aboard and down the wide aisle of the deck. She made for the portal that led inside but Esmé broke away and darted to the railing. She clung to it and stared out over the dawn-washed waterfront.

For a moment Mab stared at her daughter, so slight and slim, head back, hair chopped, long white neck so newly exposed. The fixed fascination on her face made her almost seem to glow. She reached up and slid her eye patch back. Her blue eye glittered like glass. She gasped and pointed. 'Mama! There!'

Frantically Mab followed her pointing finger, and at the same instant that she heard the first bewildered screams coming from the docks, she saw them. Black, rushing, huge. With a cry, she clawed Esmé's hands off the rail and dragged her through the doorway. She drew her step by struggling step down the corridor. Esmé lagged and looked back over her shoulder, transfixed.

They went down steps, down corridors. The ship was a labyrinth. The howls that had gone mute when they first plunged inside now filled the passages with unearthly echoes. The wolves were inside. Wild, Mab found a small empty room, pulled Esmé into it, and pushed the heavy door closed.

It didn't latch. It had no lock. Desperate, Mab drew a ragged breath and threw her back against it, just as a great weight hammered it from the outside, slamming it into the back of her head. It lurched open a crack. A black snout appeared and wolf breath steamed into the small room. With a scream Mab threw herself back against the door, fighting it, her feet scrabbling and sliding as the wolves snarled and lunged at it.

Esmé stood before her in a kind of trance.

And behind her, in the tiny dim chamber that had, an instant earlier, been empty, there appeared a figure. A voice, soft and accusing, asked, 'Where did you think you were going, Mab?'

Mab gasped, 'You!' as the figure stepped from the shadows.

He was beautiful and bestial, tall, with dark hair gleaming in riverine channels over his thick shoulders, and he gazed at Mab through the pale, terrible eyes of a Druj. He looked exactly the same as he had fourteen years ago. The same as he would look forever. He reached for Esmé and gently cupped the nape of her bare neck.

'Don't touch her!' Mab screamed at him. An impact at the door thrust her forward and she had to throw herself back, watching helplessly as the hunter turned Esmé to face him.

Esmé scarcely knew where she was. Coming out of the fugue of the wolfsong, she would not have been surprised to find herself in the snow, standing beside a quick, dark river. Indeed, she half expected it. A flood of memories had transported her to just such a place and, looking up into the eyes of the Druj hunter before her, she half believed she really was in the mountains a continent away, in memories a lifetime past. She knew this face. She had tasted these lips. She heard herself purr, 'Mihai,' in a stranger's voice, and, hearing herself, her eyes flew open wide. So did his. They stared at each other, startled.

Mab let out a sound that was like a gasp and a wail as the door battered her again and wolf snouts shoved into the crack of the door. Her feet slipped. Seeing her desperate white face, Mihai quickly whispered a word in his harsh language. A glimmering window peeled open in the air and he said, 'Come,' drawing Esmé against him with one arm and holding out his other hand to Mab. She hesitated for just a second, but then the door thrust her forward. The wolves broke through. Teeth grazed Mab's elbow. And there was Mihai clutching Esmé against his side, disappearing with her backward through the opening in the air. Mab grabbed frantically at his outstretched hand and disappeared too.

FIVE

Whispering

Druj magic must be spoken aloud. Most commonly it's whispered. The magic is in the breath, and the shape of the breath as pressed by lips, tongue, and teeth into words determines the shape of the magic. It is an important peculiarity that only the mouth of a Druj in human cithra is physiologically fit to shape language. Thus, a Druj can shift shape, but once shifted must trust to another to whisper him back again or risk eternity as a crow, owl, stag, fox, magpie, viper, or in the case of the Naxturu, a wolf.

Being alone and in exile, Mihai no longer shifted shape. There were other Druj in the cities, but they were rootless and wayward and didn't trust one another as whisperers. That was what tribes were for, and Mihai had broken from his tribe long ago. So he kept to his human cithra and used his magic for other things.

The window he whispered open in the air led straight back to Mab and Esmé's living room in London, so they tumbled from a ship in harbor in the south of France onto their own rug with as little fanfare as if they were crossing a threshold. Mab and Esmé gasped and spun around. A wolf was lunging after them and Mihai had to grab its huge jaws with both hands and wrestle it back as the glimmering window slammed shut. His hands were bleeding when he pulled them out but he took no notice.

He whirled toward the chandelier and yanked down the two long red braids, one in each bloody hand, and threw them onto the carpet. He looked at Mab, his eyes narrow. 'You should have gone to Yazad if you were afraid, Mab. Didn't I say he would always help you?' he demanded. 'Didn't I say *I* would?'

Mab didn't answer. She was gasping for breath, on the edge of hysteria.

Mihai turned to Esmé and knelt in front of her. 'Do you know who I am?' he asked softly.

She stared at him, at his fangs, at the lips that she knew from some alien tangle of memories. But it wasn't her memory! She had never kissed this creature. She had never kissed anyone! 'No,' she lied, shrinking away from him. 'I don't know you!'

He stared at her blue eye and Esmé was sure he knew she was lying. He turned again to Mab and asked her, almost gently, 'Are you hurt?'

She shook her head and tried to edge nearer to Esmé. 'I thought we were safe,' she whispered.

Mihai reached out and took her hands in his, keeping himself between mother and daughter. He kissed Mab's knuckles and she tensed as if she were afraid he might suddenly savage her. 'You *are* safe,' he told her.

'But the wolves—'

'It isn't what you think.'

'How do you know what I think?'

'I know, Mab. I was there when it happened to you, remember? This . . . isn't that.'

Mab blinked. 'Then what is it?'

'Nothing so terrible. It will be all right soon,' Mihai replied.

'But how did they find us, and why wasn't the Queen with them? What's wrong with Esmé's eye? And how did she know your name?' Mab asked in a rush.

'Everything will be all right. Soon.'

'You keep saying "soon." Isn't it all right *now*?'

'I'm sorry, Mab,' he told her, meaning it with a regret unknown to other Druj. 'I'll bring her back to you. I promise.'

'Bring her—' Mab stared at him, stricken. 'No!' She lunged toward Esmé.

But Mihai caught both her fine wrists in one hand and held her off as easily as if she were a gossamer. 'It isn't what you think,' he said again. Then he whispered open a window in the floor. Silent and surprised, Esmé dropped through it. For a frozen moment Mab saw into the impossible aperture. She saw the top of Esmé's shorn head, and she saw spires and bridges, cliff walls, drifting mist. She started to scream.

'Go to Yazad, Mab,' Mihai said, and he dove after Esmé. 'He'll explain.' The air closed around his feet, and Mab went on screaming, caught in a nightmare from which there was no waking. She only left off screaming when her voice was ravaged to a rasp, then she slumped over, panting, staring in a daze at the carpet. Only one red braid lay coiled there. Mihai had taken the other.

The Queen's Pet

Druj live forever and have forever lived. There are no new Druj, no young Druj, no ripe bellies, no babes. If their race began as infants, that history was lost in ancient books, swallowed by fire or mold. As for their memories, they have proven unfit for immortality. They recede into a lake of mist, revealing nothing. They have no legends, not even of a time before the forests grew. Nothing has ever been new, least of all themselves. To an ancient folk dulled by eternity, children are a revelation.

That's why they keep them as pets.

Mab was born in the citadel of Tajbel to a girl-mother like she herself would later become. She never knew her. The Queen's human pets were released once they gave birth to their successor, or so Mab was told. Whether all those girl-mothers were really turned loose with their pockets full of jewels, she couldn't guess. Perhaps they did walk out across the black meadows and into a new life. Or perhaps they were fed to the beasts. You never knew what the Druj might do.

They might sing to you one moment and stick you in the cage the next.

'Little sparrow, my little kit, my downy little owlet,' the Druj Queen sang to baby Mab. And though Mab didn't remember it herself, later the handmaidens would tell her that for the first few years of her life the Queen had scarcely ever set her down but carried her everywhere like a treasure, rocking her and dancing with her, and whispering made-up songs into her tiny ears, never the same lyrics twice.

She wasn't Mab then. She was called Izha and she grew up thinking that was her name. It wasn't until later, after Mihai had helped her to escape, that she found out what it meant. Mihai brought her to an old man in London – Yazad – to await Esmé's birth and learn how to be human, and Yazad had refused to call her Izha. He told her gently that it wasn't a name, but a title. It meant 'milk sacrifice' and it was what the Queen called all her girl pets, one after the next. Yazad called her simply 'dear girl' and waited for her to name herself, and once she learned to read, she did. She found a line in a poem in Yazad's marvelous library. It went, 'I am the Fairy Mab: to me 'tis given the wonders of the human world to keep,' and at that moment she became Mab.

But first she was Izha, and she belonged to the Queen.

Since leaving Tajbel, Mab had never seen a mortal woman whose beauty could touch that of the Druj Queen. She was goddess-like in her perfection, the golden glow of her skin, the facets of her sculpted lips, her face the flawless oval of a cabochon, its delicate bones a perfect counterpoint to the vivid ferocity of her gaze. Her black hair was as soft as the furs she slept on, and her flesh was as cold as river stones. Even when she held Mab in her arms, the child's human heat didn't transfer to the ice of her own skin.

She seemed to have no name. The other Druj called her Sraeshta, 'most beautiful,' and Rathaeshtar, 'warrior,' and Mazishta, 'greatest.' Mab was taught to call her Ba'thrishva.

Mother.

It was hard later to admit it, but she had adored her then, the tall, beautiful creature who held her on her hip, so easy in the crook of one long arm. She had even loved her eyes and thought they were like the blue jewels in the frame of the great milky mirror in her Tabernacle of Spies. Mab's own eyes reflected in that same mirror could only seem wrong, since no one else had brown eyes, not even the lowest Druj handmaidens. Brown eyes seemed *animal*, as unprecious as bone buttons or an owl's talon on a leather cord.

From her earliest awareness, Mab understood that she was not Druj. She didn't have blue eyes and cold skin. She couldn't shift shape, or fly, or slip suddenly invisible. She didn't know *what* she was, but she guessed she must be animal, like one of the cats that were everywhere in Tajbel, or like the forest creatures – though perhaps a rare and special one, as there were no others like her, and the Queen seemed to treasure her above all else. For a time, anyway.

She sang, 'Hair like fire and skin like snow and eyes as brown as a forest doe,' and she kissed Mab's small nose and breathed the scent of her hair. She taught her to dance, embroider, play the kamanchay, and mix herbs into a tea that would keep her always healthy. She dressed her in strange and beautiful clothes, and she wove intricate crowns of flowers for her hair. One summer she showed her how to fish for butterflies off the cliff's edge. Together they would bait their lines with blossoms and wait quietly for butterflies to alight on them and then slowly, slowly, they would reel them in, and the Queen would reach out, take them onto her finger, and transfer them to Mab's hair, where they would perch, fanning their wings in the sun like a crown of living flowers. Once, she fashioned a harness out of deer hide and commanded her handmaidens to shift to owl cithrim and carry Mab up into the sky, a little girl borne aloft by a dozen soundless wings.

It was from there, on high, that Mab had her only glimpse of the greater world. Tajbel was a place lost in mountains, as hidden as a vein of gold. It was a citadel of spires, each carved from immense, tapering tusks of rock that rose from a chasm so deep that echoes lost their way in it and drowned in its silence. The tusks were connected by dozens of bridges, and more bridges arced gracefully toward the canyon walls, where cliff-cut stairs rose to the forest above. There – the dappled edge of the trees – was the boundary of Mab's known world.

When the handmaidens flew her into the sky, she witnessed the immeasurable sweep of the forest-flocked mountains rising and falling as far as she could see, and the immensity was beyond anything she could have dreamed. That, then, was the world: mountain and forest, forever. She never imagined another landscape. She never fathomed a *beyond*. Even later, when life devolved into misery, she didn't dream of escape – she knew there was nowhere to go. It would take more than misery before she would finally attempt it.

But that was later. When she was small, Mab was happy, much of the time.

She slept in the Queen's chamber with her, on her own little bed of furs at the foot of the Queen's own. In the summer she was given nectar in a little dish to lap at with her tongue, in winter icicles rolled in sugar to suck. The Queen stroked her hair when it was warmed by the sun, and swaddled her in wool and furs against the cold.

If she sometimes grew bored, if that flat, reptilian look of utter disinterest came into her eyes and she shooed Mab away, surely it was Mab's own fault for being dull, lesser, *animal*. And the cage, surely that was her own fault too.

It was an iron cage and it hung off the side of the Queen's bridge in view of her windows, and sometimes she would put Mab in it and leave her there. Its iron suspension rings ground together and shrieked if she moved, which is how Mab learned to hold so very, very still. She also learned to hate the breeze that set the cage swaying in spite of her stillness, because the screech of the iron drew the notice of the beasts, and she could see their phosphorescent eyes watching her from beneath the bridges, coolly considering her in her swinging cage.

She would never forget those eyes, or the rank smell the wind teased up from under the bridges, and she would never forget the silhouettes of the beasts' long, white arms reaching up to grope for any live thing they might pull down into their gaping mouths – cats, a fawn . . . *her*. The Queen had forbidden them to touch her, but they were beasts after all, and they had disobeyed her before.

The Queen liked to watch the beasts watch Mab. It amused her, the risk of it.

Mab never knew just what the beasts were, or how many there were – one to each bridge, or a mere handful creeping in the darkness from one bridge to the next, or perhaps an ever-shifting multitude of them that scaled up from the depths of the chasm below when they were hungry. And they were always hungry.

That's what the cats were for.

'Look, Izha has a kitty,' observed a handmaiden one day on the steps of the Queen's spire. Her name was Snaya and she was often in charge of Mab, leading her hither and thither by a little leather thong tied around her wrist. She gave the thong a yank and Mab tried to pull away. She clutched the kitten in her arms and instinctively curled around it to protect it. She must have been about three years old then, but she knew the fate of cats in Tajbel.

'No,' she whispered.

The kitten was a tabby, long-haired and soft. It had been purring but stopped at the sound of Snaya's voice. Its tiny claws stabbed Mab's arms as it tried, suddenly, to scramble away. She held on, wincing at the scratches. She should have let it go.

'Come here, Izha, pretty pet,' Snaya coaxed. Her voice was sweet, but her grip on the leather thong was not. She gave it a hard tug that burned the skin of Mab's wrist and Mab tumbled toward her, slipping over the steep, rock-cut steps and into the handmaiden's arms.

Snaya scooped her up, kitten and all, and carried her to the foot of the bridge. 'Go on, Izha, toss it,' she ordered.

'No!' said Mab, holding the kitten close. It hissed and struggled against her chest.

'Now,' said Snaya through clenched teeth.

But Mab would not throw the kitten and so Snaya, gripping fistfuls of Mab's shift, slowly swung her out over the bridge. She heard a gurgle of phlegmy breathing coming from the shadows. Great flat teeth ground together.

And Snaya dropped her.

Or, for a hovering instant, it seemed that she had. Mab seemed to hang there in the air, and she knew that in another second she would land on the bridge and the beast would get her. In a panic she loosed her grip on the kitten and it dropped – but Mab did not. Snaya caught her by the hair and clothes and dragged her back to safety.

The kitten landed on its feet, took a tottering step, then another. Bewildered, it looked back at Mab with its big golden eyes, and then there was a flash of long white arm through the balusters and it was gone.

A pitiable mewl, a crunch, a waft of stench. The beast ate, and while it was thus distracted, Snaya carried Mab across the bridge with light, dancing steps.

The cats were toll for bridge crossings.

'Like you, pretty, the beasts must eat,' said Snaya, and even as a tiny thing, Mab had heard the disdain in her voice and understood its meaning. Druj did *not* eat. They occasionally sipped wine from carved goblets, but eating was for animals.

That night, Mab woke screaming for the first time in her life and the Queen came and picked her up and rocked her. Mab wept, and her Ba'thrishva took the opportunity to taste the tears on her cheeks. Her tongue was as cold as the rest of her flesh, but her rocking was calming, and she hummed in Mab's ear to quiet her. 'Izha, sweetest,' she said. 'Tell me what happened.'

Mab told. She showed the Queen the kitten scratches and the welt around her wrist from the leather thong, and Snaya was punished. The Queen made her shift to cat cithra and she left her like that. She refused to whisper her back and Snaya had to live as a cat for weeks, dodging the groping arms of the beasts. Sometimes the Queen would pick her up and stand stroking her black fur at the threshold of the bridge as if considering tossing her onto it.

No one tormented Mab after that, except for the Queen herself.

At first it was only neglect, and like everything else, it was Mab's own fault. She *grew*. She outgrew the little iron cage and wasn't sorry for that, but she also outgrew her place on her Ba'thrishva's hip, and day by day the Queen seemed to have less use for her. Mab's little bed of furs was moved out of the Queen's chamber and into a desolate stairwell in the back of the spire. No one fed her – as the Druj didn't eat, such things were easily forgotten. Mab had to sift for herself through the tithes that were gathered twice yearly from the black meadows. She was five years old when she learned about rationing. That first winter of her self-sufficiency, she ran out of food. She grew thin on a diet of moss; she ate fish raw. She ate bark.

The tithe stores were replenished in spring, and after that she was careful. She kept herself alive. Seasons passed. She spent her days in embroidery and practice at her kamanchay. She brushed her own hair now, and she made her own clothes and tried to make gifts for her Ba'thrishva too. One winter when the Queen and the Naxturu were away on their yearly hunt, she spent the months embroidering a robe with intricate birds and butterflies in a hundred colors, but the Queen never wore it, not once.

For some years during that bend in her life Mab thought she had discovered misery, but when she was older, she would look back wistfully on that time, because what came after made it seem almost sweet by comparison.

One night when she was ten, her life cleaved neatly into a time *before* and a time *after*, and that subtle starvation, that neglect and loneliness, belonged to *before*, when she had still been happy.

The night was Vishaptatha. There was always a surge of energy in Tajbel on full-moon nights, and Vishaptatha wasn't just any full moon. It was also perigee, when the moon comes closest to the earth in its celestial sweep and waxes huge in the heavens. Vishaptatha occurs rarely; many years may pass without a full moon coinciding with perigee. This was the first of Mab's life and she felt the thrill of it, the thrum. The Druj seemed to be waiting for something to happen, so she waited too.

And something did happen.

The handmaidens came to her as they used to when she was still the Queen's treasure. They brushed out her long red hair, dressed her in a wondrous sheath of spider silk and seed pearls, and brought her to the small plateau atop the Queen's tusk. The Queen was there, wearing a shimmering silken sheath of her own, and no sooner had the handmaidens delivered Mab than they shed their own robes and became owls, scattering to the night on silent wings. All throughout Tajbel the Druj were shifting. The Naxturu were howling and foxes were barking; there was a chitter and chirrup of birds, the stamp of deer hooves, and the low, dangerous throat-yowls of snow leopards. Only the Queen did not shift. She never did.

Standing in the streaming light of the huge moon, she beckoned Mab toward her and Mab went, willing. With a pounding heart she yearned toward her Ba'thrishva, hoping for a caress. It had been so long since she'd been touched. The Queen slid one finger under Mab's chin and tilted her head up. Mab smiled, uncertain.

It was the last time she would look at those pale eyes without the ice of dread crystallizing within her.

'Izha,' whispered the Queen, her fangs glittering.

Then the cold rushed in and filled Mab's being. It was like drowning in snowmelt, blind, dizzy, and breathless. She was shoved deep inside herself, muffled, stifled, and the shock was so great she was scarcely aware her body went on moving through the long moonstruck night. Her arms and legs were no longer her own. Her eyes were not hers either, but she caught glimpses out of them and it was like peering through a kaleidoscope of shadows. She saw the Queen's body standing vacant, her eyes as dead as glass. She saw wheeling owls, and the silhouettes of wolves howling on the peaks of the far spires. She saw herself in the Queen's mirror. It was her own small face in the reflection – those were her own brown eyes, but she wasn't alone in peering out of them.

She had a trespasser. She was crushed down inside herself, tamped down, creased, torn, bruised. That first time the Queen entered her, Mab knew little else but her shock, little but the cold and the ache, but she would soon grow accustomed to it. It was the new shape of her life.

In the weeks, months, and years that followed, Mab learned that she was even less than she had always thought. She wasn't animal. She was *cithra*. She was just something for the Queen to wear, like a robe, like a fur. She would watch the Queen's empty body from within her own violated one, would see the stillness of that empty vessel and wish her own self might be a sacred place, a clean and empty cloister unscuffed by trespassers.

The next years went slowly by, and then Mab's bleeding came, and again everything changed.

SEVEN

Stained

One dawn in her fourteenth year, Mab woke stained on her bed of white fox pelts, and she didn't understand. She knew blood – she had seen the Naxturu slit deer bellies and spill them out, and she'd seen cats' whiskers tinged red after a meal of voles or songbirds. Blood meant death, and somehow it had gotten into bed with her. She touched between her legs and her fingers came away red. It was her own blood!

In her terror she searched for a wound and found none, only the folds of herself as they had always been, and then she thought she must have done some new nasty thing that the Druj didn't do, something animal and foul. She shuddered. Never did she feel lower than when she had to creep out to the trees and squat like an animal to make waste.

She rose, furtive, hoping to slip out of the tower and across the bridge, to make her way unseen into the forest to cleanse herself of the bewildering shame of her blood. It had flowed onto the fox pelts too, and she gathered up the top few and took them with her down the long, curved stairs to the Queen's bridge.

She hesitated there and looked from side to side along the chasm of Tajbel. Mist hung heavy in the air and the spires were dusky purple through the haze. Some curved like the horns of sheep, others stood straight as knives. There were windows in them, glassless, and Mab knew the Druj slept dreamlessly just out of view. She was desperate not to wake them. She regarded the bridge before her.

She knew better than to traipse across without an offering for the beasts. She could smell them, the thick rot of them, and in the fogged silence of the dawn she could even hear the wheezing breath of one as it waited in the shadows. She looked around. There were no cats near, and she was glad of it. In her urgency she might have scooped one up and tossed it out onto the bridge. Disgusted by the thought, she clutched the fox pelts and tried not to cry.

The fox pelts. She looked down at them, considering. Surely the beast would smell her blood on them; it would smell blood and feel fur and for a moment it might be fooled. Not once the dead fur was in its mouth, crunchless and spurtless, but for a moment – enough time for Mab to race across the bridge. So she hurled the two pelts, and as soon as the beast's long arm groped through the balusters of the bridge to seize them and drag them down, she took to her toes and ran.

Her feet scarcely touched stone as she raced across, fearing at any second to feel a big rotten hand wrap round her leg. But she made it and shot up the steps on the far side, up the last lip of cliff and into the forest, and when she felt pine needles under her feet, she slowed. Behind her the beast bellowed, displeased with its dead mouthful, and she trembled and went to the stream. Deer were there drinking; they didn't mind her soft steps, but just looked at her and kept on as she knelt on the bank and plunged her stained fingers into the cold water.

The cold felt pure. Mab stripped off her thin shift and slipped into the stream, wading out to the middle where the water came to her waist. She scrubbed herself and dunked her head under too, so her hair was a red cloud around her, then she climbed out and sat shivering on a flat rock as the sun finished rising. The deer moved off. Mab slipped her shift back on and returned to Tajbel, waiting at the foot of the bridge until Snaya found her and paid the toll with a ginger cat.

The rest of the morning went like any other. She ate some wild apples and worked the knots out of her hair with her ivory comb. She tried to do some embroidery, but the piece she was working on was red thread on white muslin and reminded her of her blood. She put it away, shoving the mystery of her bleeding to the back of her mind and hoping to leave it there. It was over, she thought. *Over.*

But it came again, and this time there was no hiding it. She was playing her kamanchay when the Queen, passing her doorway, suddenly stopped and spun toward her. The sudden movement made Mab flinch and she sawed her bow across the strings, producing a sound like a moan. The Queen was staring at her, her icy eyes aglitter and unnaturally bright. She said, 'Izha, you're *bleeding.*'

'No—' protested Mab.

'I can smell it.'

Mab's breath caught in her throat. She dropped the kamanchay with a clatter and tried backing away on her knees, but the Queen said, 'Stop,' and she did.

'I'm sorry . . .' she whispered. 'I didn't mean to—'

The Queen came to her and Mab flinched again and squeezed her eyes shut. But the touch that she felt on her hair was very, very soft, just fingertips trailing over the curve of her skull, and when the

Queen spoke again, her voice was like a purr. 'Child, child, stand up. It's all right. I've been waiting a long time for this. Look at me.'

Look at me. It was a command that sent a chill down Mab's spine; whenever she heard it, she knew what would come next – the Queen's animus flooding into her like black water. Trembling, she looked up into those pale eyes. She waited for the cold but it didn't come. The Queen didn't slide inside her, but only stared at her, that queer glitter still bright in her eyes, her lips curved into a kind of amazed smile. Again she stroked Mab's hair, and it felt nice, like it had in that before time when Mab had been a little creature in her lap, pretty and petted.

'It's the vohunish, child, the life-making blood,' she said. 'Don't be afraid. Smile for me. There.'

Mab's smile was a grimace, but the Queen cared little for the distinction between real emotions and feigned ones. She clapped for her handmaidens and when they came, she announced, 'Our Izha has grown up!'

Grown up. How little those words had meant to Mab then! Surrounded by changeless Druj, what did she have to go on? Kittens growing long and lean? Deer sprouting antlers to clash in the rut? Later, she would look back and wonder how she hadn't guessed what was coming. It would seem to her that the gathering doom should have blotted out all else, like thunderheads roiling before the sun, but there had been nothing like that, only a small, pathetic hope that the Queen might love her again. *Love!* As if the Druj were capable of it! She herself didn't even know the word then, scarcely knew the feeling. But she would learn it.

At the Queen's announcement, the handmaidens seemed to

thrum with that same cold species of excitement that had overtaken them on Vishaptatha, and a throbbing dread filled Mab. Something was going to happen. She knew it. But whatever it was, it didn't happen, and it didn't happen, and her dread stretched itself out fine and taut across the weeks of autumn. Her bleeding came and went twice more, and she waited and waited for the new bad thing, but still it didn't come.

In fact, those months were sweet. The Queen cherished her again and kept her close, and the handmaidens fluttered around her like birds, petting her with their hands as soft as owl feathers. The tithes had just been gathered, so there was fresh food in plenty, cheeses and dried cherries and strips of meat, more than usual and all for her. She was never hungry that autumn and she began to put on flesh, a little, so she was no longer sharp in the ribs and knees like a fawn. Her breasts grew. Her hips fluted out. Every day the handmaidens rubbed scented oils into her skin until she was pink and fragrant, and they sang her a song about ripening fruit that she had never heard.

'Grapes on the vine, lips as sweet as cherries, nectar dark as wine, ripen, sweet fruit, ripen. Plums that I can gather, swelling on the branches, ripen, orchard, ripen. Ripen, berry, ripen.'

The Queen sang too, and her voice was sweeter than anyone's, but through all the petting and the singing, Mab never lost her dread. Perhaps it was the way Isvant the hunter looked at her now, with something in his eyes that made her want to cover herself. Her own nakedness had never meant anything to her before; she was as a bird before the Druj, or a fish. Her skin was her self, only to be hidden against the cold. But one day Isvant came as a crow to perch in her rock window and watched the handmaidens anoint her with their oils, and even in crow cithra his look was like a leer. She shivered and crossed her arms over her small breasts and he cawed an ugly laugh and kept on watching. Snaya laughed too and sang, 'Fruit sweet for the plucking, ripen, berry, ripen.'

Mab was grateful when the season's first snow fell that night, because it meant the Queen and the Naxturu would be going away.

The Boy

Izha, wake up,' said the Queen. She was kneeling at Mab's bed-side, and even before Mab opened her eyes, she smelled the snow in the air and knew what was coming. *Peace* was coming. Months of it.

'Snow,' she murmured, sitting up in her furs.

'Snow,' said the Queen.

The first snow always heralded the Winter Hunt. The Queen would take her Naxturu and go away. They would stalk the forest, cleansing it of poachers, and they would range far, visiting distant Druj tribes to reassert the Queen's rule over them all. She always brought back silky pelts and strange seed pods, jewels and silver-work and wine, and in her pockets, wrapped in leaves, she carried home a tender cargo of freshly plucked eyeballs to add to the collection in her Tabernacle of Spies.

They were away for months each year, and when Mab was small, those months had been lonely, but after that fateful Vishaptatha she had learned to welcome them. She spent her winters cold to the bone and huddled in furs, but at peace in her body and blessedly alone.

'Let me braid your hair, my pretty child,' said the Queen, and Mab turned and sat still while the Queen brushed out her hair and plaited and twisted it into long graceful spirals all down her bare back. It took several hours. She hummed the whole time, that same strange ripening song, and when she was done, she drew a curved knife from a sheath at her hip and sliced off one braid, which she tied to the chain of the moonstone amulet she wore always around her neck. Then she kissed Mab on the brow with her icy lips and left.

From the window Mab watched the Naxturu assume wolf cithrim. There were six of them, three male, three female, and they dropped their cloaks in the snow and stood for an instant naked before their bodies hunched over and attenuated, sprouted black fur, ears, tails. Each wolf howled once and turned to face the Queen. As ever, the Queen did not change.

'Can't she?' Mab had asked Snaya once, long ago.

Snaya had made a scornful sound in her throat and replied, 'Of course she can! Mazishta could change into the moon itself if she wished.'

Then why didn't she? Mab had wondered. It was such a marvelous thing that the Druj could do. If the Queen was most powerful of all of them, why did she not do it too? That last winter in Tajbel, she still didn't know. She watched a low-caste Druj ready the Queen's sledge, test the edges of its long, curved runners, and harness the bezoar goats that would pull it. They were fantastical creatures and huge, with scimitar horns sharp enough to slit throats, and when the Queen gave a whistle, they were off and stamping. Snow flew. The wolves howled. The Queen looked back over her shoulder once and Mab saw her eyes flash like sunstruck ice and she glimpsed her own red braid fastened at the Queen's perfect throat.

And then she was gone, and the winter stretched ahead like a field of untrammeled snow. Peace.

Of course, it couldn't last. As she did every year, the Queen
returned. But Mab soon learned this year was not like every year.
Not anything like. She woke one dawn to find the Queen bending
over her just as on the morning she'd left. She blinked awake. Was
the winter already over? The Queen's eyes were bright.

'Izha, a surprise,' she said, her voice husky. 'Come.'

She led her from her bed and scrubbed her with handfuls of
snow, too impatient even to let it melt into water first. The handmaidens fluttered around her but didn't touch her. This morning,
more than ever, Mab belonged to the Queen. She rubbed Mab's skin
with oils, and then she did something new. She painted her flesh. A
handmaiden named Keshva brought a squirrel-hair brush and a pot
of indigo paint and the Queen took them and drew blue coils around
Mab's arms and legs, and spirals around her navel and breasts. At
the base of her throat she painted three small symbols: the moon
waxing, full, and waning. As she drew them, Mab saw the handmaidens' eyes over the top of the Queen's bent head. Her heartbeat
quickened. Their eyes, they were like the eyes of cats watching the
futile scuttling of injured prey as they toyed with it, minute by minute, prolonging for pleasure the inevitable fatal strike.

And she knew this was the moment her dread had reached for,
all those months ago.

The Queen rose and led Mab to the window, where they
watched several low-caste Druj toss cats to the beasts until they were
sated. Then, from across the bridge came a short procession. Isvant
was at the head of it, and beside him, stumbling, was a boy. Mab
stared. In all her life she had never seen another human being, but
still, a thrill of instant recognition sparked through her. The boy
was naked as she was, and his arms and legs were ringed in blue paint

too. She couldn't take her eyes off him. Looking at him was like seeing evidence that she herself truly existed, that she wasn't only a
cithra for the Queen to wear, but something *alive* and *distinct*.

And she understood why the Queen had taken her braid on the
Winter Hunt. The boy's hair was the exact same shade as her own,
red as persimmons, and like hers his skin was the color of cream,
unsprinkled by the spice of freckles. To look at them, they might
have been brother and sister.

Isvant pushed the boy up the rock steps and into the chamber
to where Mab stood beside the Queen. All the Druj followed. They
crowded in and nudged him toward her, that queer, predatory glitter
in their eyes. The boy was shaking and Mab began to shake too. She
didn't understand what they wanted her to do. For a terrible moment
she was afraid they'd make her kill him like a cat and shove his body
to the beasts. Panic rose in her. Her eyes darted between the Queen's
icy gaze and Isvant's leer and found no answer and no comfort. All
the others stood watching, and for an instant Mab's eyes fell on a
stranger's face among all the familiar ones. As alike as Druj were,
she knew them all, and this one was not from Tajbel.

It wasn't just that he was a stranger that made her gaze falter on
his face; it was the look that flickered through his eyes, a kind of
look Mab had never seen on a Druj before. She only knew it from
seeing it in her own reflection. It was *pain*.

Then the Queen set her finger beneath Mab's chin and raised
up her face. That blaze of blue, the feeling of falling into a freezing
river, and everything became muted and distant. The Queen was
inside of her and Mab was as powerless over her own body as if she
were merely its shadow. Dimly she saw her own painted arms reaching for the boy, but she could barely feel his skin beneath her

fingertips. It was the Queen who felt what her fingers felt as she traced them over his sharp young clavicles, his heartbeat in his thin chest as clear and fast as a bird's.

Then his trembling ceased at once and his face went blank, and Mab knew that brutal Isvant had gone inside of him. The boy's hand reached out to grip Mab's wrist in just the way that Isvant did when he pulled her across a bridge, as if she were only a corpse he had to haul from one place to another.

He – the boy, but not the boy – pulled her down on the furs. Captured inside herself as she had been so many times, Mab turned aside and waited. She was only an unformed thing within a chrysalis, and she no more felt the flesh on her flesh than a butterfly pupa feels rain on its cocoon. She waited for it to be over, and in time it was. But before it was, she noticed the new Druj again in the throng of watchers and she fixed on his face. It shone out from the others, rigid as it was, as if this stranger held a struggling thing between his teeth and had to champ down until it died. The struggling thing, Mab was certain, was indeed pain, though she knew Druj felt it not. It was a mystery. *He* was a mystery, and he gave her something to wonder about until the Queen and Isvant finished their charade and returned to their own bodies.

The Queen's body stirred. She lifted her chin and turned coolly away from Mab, leaving her lying on the furs, her blue paint smeared and mixed with the boy's blue paint. He was weeping quietly beside her and Mab slowly came back to herself to turn to him and stroke his hair and murmur to him, and the Queen stopped and looked back over her shoulder to watch. A flicker of annoyance passed over her face.

Mab met her eyes boldly and went on stroking the boy's hair, amazed by the heat of his brow. She understood several new things at once. One was that she wasn't alone in the world, but one of a mysterious species that existed elsewhere. The other was that whatever she was, in some way, the Queen coveted it. Druj could wear borrowed bodies against each other, but they would feel only the friction of it. They would never feel what it was that made two strangers cling to each other, more intimate in fear and sorrow than a Druj could ever be, even aping the act of love.

Mab understood then that the Druj were missing something. It was Yazad, later, who would explain about souls. She couldn't have put any of it into words then, lying on those furs with the boy, but even without the words, she began to understand.

Many months later, when she felt the first flutter of life within her and her hands flew to her belly, that understanding focused into a hard, bright point within her, like a pearl. Here was something else the Druj couldn't do, she thought fiercely. And though the Queen could flow inside of her and steal the feeling of that flutter for herself, Mab knew that the pearl inside her was her own, and nothing the Queen ever did could change that.

And she knew that she could never walk out across the black meadows with empty arms, buying her freedom with the tiny life inside her. She thought of the lineage of girl-mothers who had come before her and she tried to imagine them leaving Tajbel and going away, emptied of their babies, empty as eggshells, and she just couldn't believe it.

What had happened to her own mother, and all those before her?

Because of Mihai, Mab never knew, and because of him, her daughter never had to endure starvation, or the cage, or the sinister thrust of a Druj animus. For some reason, he had saved them. So when he stole Esmé away and Mab glimpsed the rough spires of Tajbel through his window of air, all the old agonies overwhelmed her and she screamed until she could scream no more, and then she collapsed onto the rug, rigid. She was seeing young limbs encircled by blue paint and hearing in her mind a song about ripening fruit. She clutched at her flat stomach, long empty of its precious pearl, and she imagined gentle Esmé being led to a stolen boy of her own, to breed the Queen a red-haired pet that human arms would never hold.

'It isn't what you think,' Mihai had said, but Mab was trapped in nightmares and could dream no other fate.

· NINE ·

City of Beasts

Mihai's whispered window spilled Esmé onto a narrow stone bridge. She landed on her knees and spun swiftly around. Mihai was right behind her, and she glimpsed her mother's desperate hands and heard her screams until the air sealed itself shut once more and choked off her voice. The profound silence that followed was akin to deafness.

Esmé crawled backward. She pressed herself against the carved balusters of the bridge and watched Mihai. He was standing with his hands on his hips, slowly looking around. A cold wind whipped his hair into his eyes and impatiently he pushed it back. There was a look of ill-concealed horror on his face and Esmé looked to see what he was seeing. The bridge they had landed on spanned the space between two tall crags of rock. Worn stone steps spiraled up and around the towers and disappeared into passages, and glassless windows revealed barren rooms inside. There were many such crags rising like stalagmites from the shadow-shrouded depths of a long ravine. They tapered up to conical spires, ridged like animal horns, and they tapered downward too as if they had grown up from the blackness below on long stone stalks, dangerously delicate.

This landscape looked as if it had been disgorged by the mountains themselves, as if it were the earth's own elemental imitation of the castles built by men. It was an otherworldly place and Esmé felt a tingling of recognition at odds with her awe for its alien strangeness. 'Where are we?' she asked Mihai.

He turned sharply and gave her a penetrating look. 'I think you know,' he said.

And she realized she did. 'Tajbel,' she whispered. The word formed on her lips like something she had always known.

'What's left of it,' Mihai said, and Esmé read shock in his eyes. He turned in a slow circle and murmured words that Esmé had heard Mab speak. '*Avo afritim*. Bless and protect us.'

Even she could sense that something was wrong here. The citadel seemed deserted. Cold wind coursed among the spires but made almost no sound. A drapery of vines claimed the bridges and chasm walls, and in many places the finely carved stone was crumbling away. One whole bridge had collapsed into the black, leaving only a few feet of stonework on either side, like walkways to nothingness. 'Who lives here?' Esmé asked. 'Where are they all?'

Mihai didn't answer. He suddenly tensed and tilted back his head like a predator scenting the air. Then his eyes widened and he spun toward Esmé, dropping to a crouch and shooting out one hand to grab her ankle and drag her to him. It was all one fluid motion, and Esmé cried out, startled, and tried to twist away. But before she even knew what was happening, Mihai had hooked one arm around her waist, too tight, and hoisted her off her feet. She saw a blade glint as he drew a knife from some hidden sheath, but she hadn't even time to gasp before he leapt with animal grace up onto the narrow balustrade of the bridge, upon which he balanced with Esmé still in his grasp.

She started to struggle but then a smell of rot hit her, and an arm, thick, white as fish, scab-pocked and horrifically long, swung up from beneath the bridge to pummel the stretch of railing against which, a second earlier, she had been leaning. The whole bridge trembled and the balusters shattered like icicles. Blunt, clawed fingers scrabbled through the shards, searching, searching for flesh. For Esmé.

Finding nothing, the beast swung its other arm onto the bridge and hauled itself up into the light of day. Esmé gasped. Its eyes bulged and glowed yellow over a flat nose, little more than slits on a nub of dead-looking flesh. Its whole squat head appeared to be no more than an anchor for the massive bones and muscles required to work its jaw. Esmé watched in horrified fascination as its mouth opened huge to reveal rows of flat, worn teeth and a gullet wide enough to swallow animals whole. It bellowed and Esmé heard herself shriek. Holding her, Mihai backed up along the railing, graceful as a cat, and the beast shambled after them.

'What is that?' she asked urgently.

The bridge shuddered again and Mihai swung to look behind him, spinning Esmé in an arc that revealed to her a panorama of Tajbel's bridges one after the next all through the long ravine. She gasped. From beneath each bridge she saw them coming, scrambling. Up from the blackness, arm over long arm, quick and desperate, coming. They were sickly white, their skin stretched taut, cheeks and guts sunken to hollows. They were starving, Esmé realized, their huge jaws gaping as if hoping someone might toss something in. Behind Mihai another had pulled itself onto the bridge and more were coming after it, crushing the fine stone balusters in their haste.

Again, frantic, she asked, 'What are they?'

Mihai glanced at her, taking his attention from the beasts for just an instant to study her. His eyes were narrowed, one eyebrow raised in a question. Only after he turned away again did he say, under his breath, 'I don't know. She would never tell.'

'She – ?' Esmé started to say, but she lost her breath when a beast lunged at them. Mihai swung his blade and severed the monster's hand from its wrist. Black blood pulsed from the stump but the beast hardly seemed to notice and kept coming.

For fourteen years the beasts had had to fend for themselves, and they had not fared well. When the cats were all gone, they'd breached the forest to hunt, but their putrid scent had chased away all prey but the sick and weak. They'd grabbed at fish in the stream; they'd resorted to cannibalism.

The scent of blood temporarily diverted the other oncoming beasts from Mihai and Esmé, and they went for their wounded fellow. Beast against beast they clashed, crazed. One knocked another off the bridge and it wailed as it fell, a long, fading ululation unpunctuated by any thud or rock slide from below. The cry just faded as if the chasm had no bottom. Jaws gaped and fingers reached as the beasts came at Mihai and Esmé from both sides.

More came. Too many more.

There sounded a great crack and the bridge lurched. It dropped a foot and Mihai kept his balance, but then it started to break apart beneath its load and crumble away into the abyss. Esmé squeezed her eyes shut and screamed, but her voice was lost in the roar of the collapsing bridge. Behind her shut eyelids she imagined the blackness of the chasm rushing up to swallow her and she thought of Mab back in London, alone, and she knew her mother wouldn't survive losing her. She felt a terrible surge of anguish and then, at once, she realized she *wasn't* falling. Mihai's arm still held her so tight she could barely breathe, and she wasn't falling. She fluttered open her eyes. The bridge and the beasts were gone – there were plenty more, to be sure, and they were still coming, but that danger seemed distant now. The bridge she had stood on had fallen away, and those beasts with it.

In Mihai's grasp, she was floating. Stunned, she looked up at him.

He was whispering fiercely and without pause. His Druj eyes looked almost white in the gloom as he stared straight ahead, whispering his magic. He and Esmé drifted through the air and Esmé's heart thudded in her chest, her mouth hanging slack in amazement. Beasts grunted and swung along the walls of the ravine, trying to reach them. Mihai carried Esmé across the chasm on gliding steps. It was like flying.

He brought her to the very last spire. It was taller than the others and had once been joined to them by a bridge, but it was clear the bridge had fallen long ago; its abutments had been swallowed by creeping vines and all that was visible was one rusted truss jutting from the vegetation. From it hung a small iron cage.

The sight of the cage thrust a spear of memory into Esmé's consciousness. It was only a glimpse, but for a split second she seemed to see long red hair spilling out through the bars, and small hands clutching at them from within. Then Mihai set her down in a portico before the lone spire's battered door. Deep claw marks scored the wood. The beasts had tried to get in here, but the door appeared intact. Mihai took a key from his pocket and fitted it into the lock. As the door swung inward, a choking odor rushed out, a fume of rot many years entombed. Esmé stumbled back and swayed at the edge of the step, overcome with nausea. It was a sheer drop to the chasm below, and Mihai reached out and gripped her arm, hard.

'Ow,' she said, as he pulled her forward into the dark reek of the spire. 'Wait,' she cried, resisting. 'I don't want to go in there—'

'The beasts will come,' Mihai said, pulling her inside and closing and locking the door behind them. Esmé thought she would suffocate in the dense, putrid air, and she dropped to her knees to retch. When she was through and looked round, Mihai had gone deeper into the rough rock chamber. It was dark, but not fully dark. A few small apertures in the rock admitted shafts of light, enough to illuminate a milky mirror framed in jewels. Esmé's memory sang to her at the sight of it. She knew the mirror. She knew this place.

It was like a chapel, the rock ceiling high and vaulted. The walls recessed into niches and were carved with the clustered shapes of winged men and stags and wolves and moons, crows and serpents and crocodile beasts with the heads of hawks. And amid the carvings Esmé saw eyelids, dozens and dozens – perhaps *hundreds* – of tarnished silver eyelids, just as she had dreamed about on her fitful night in France before the wolves found her. In her dream they had opened to reveal real eyes, but these were all closed. Viscous yellow streaks had dribbled from some of the hinged corners and Esmé realized this was the source of the smell: dead eyes, hundreds of them.

Mihai watched her. Esmé thought he seemed to expect something of her.

'What is this place . . . ?' she murmured.

'Don't you remember?' he asked softly.

Remember? She wanted to shake her head, to deny any such memories. How could she remember a chapel of silver eyelids?

How could she recognize that iron cage hanging outside? And how could she know that Mihai's lips had tasted like river? What was happening to her? In her memory things were moving. Deep, as if her mind had a crypt that had been unsealed and in it things were uncoiling – stealthy things, clammy as reptile flesh, things she didn't want to see by the light of day.

She caught a flicker of movement out of the corner of her eye and turned, freezing in place when she saw what it was. One of the eyelids had opened. They weren't all dead. The sickly orb of an eye stared out at her; its iris was brown, like her own eyes. Her *real* eyes. It seemed human. She felt pinned in place by its scrutiny and held very still, not even daring to breathe.

'It doesn't see you. That's not the way it works,' Mihai said, noticing her rigid posture. He gestured to the mirror and said, 'Watch.'

Esmé looked at the glass. Something stirred in its cloudy surface and an image began to take shape. When it cleared, she saw a line of camels swaying their way over a dune with a red sky behind them, a sinking sun, and long shadows splayed out ahead of them. For an instant she felt as if she were there, trudging with them in the sand. 'Where . . . where is that?' she asked Mihai.

'You would know better than I.'

She felt a flash of frustration. How would she know? She turned from the mirror to retort, but before she could speak, something clambered up from that seething crypt of memory and assaulted her. It was a face. A man. A man with one eye. The socket of the other was hollow and raw and Esmé's gorge rose in her throat. She shook her head and the face receded. She whispered, 'I *don't* know.'

He shrugged. 'Nor do I. Africa maybe. She had spies every-where. This is – *was* – the Tabernacle of Spies. The Druj Queen has always collected eyes. From village rats, eagles circling in the skies, crows, even songbirds in the thickets. She would take one eye and bring it here and leave the creature where it was, and she could see what her spies saw as they moved through the world. All of them. And not just animals. Humans too, like this one.' He gestured to the staring brown eye. 'She liked to watch the world.'

'She . . . she plucked out their eyeballs?' Esmé asked. 'That's . . . *terrible.*' Then she paused, struck suddenly by the memory of her mother and the one-eyed seagull on the beach years ago. Mab's behavior didn't seem so irrational now.

Mihai was looking at all the silver eyelids and all the trails of old rot that had oozed from them, and he said, 'I suppose most of the spies have died. She used to maintain her collection so care-fully, replacing old eyes with new. She won't be happy to see it like this. To see all of Tajbel fallen to this,' he said, and Esmé thought she detected not only sadness in him, but as he watched her face closely, also a hint of fear.

'Was this your city?' she asked.

'Not mine. I came from another tribe.'

'You have tribes? What . . . what *are* you?'

He looked at her keenly again, and again she had the sense he was expecting something of her. 'We are Druj,' he said simply.

'I know, but what *are* you?'

'Ah, Esmé. I haven't learned how to tell that story yet.'

'Is it true you don't have souls?'

'We never die. What need have we for souls?'

'Is that all souls are for? For when we die?' asked Esmé.

Something happened in Mihai's face then. The cool, almost cruel, animal flatness of his expression vanished and in spite of his sharp teeth and his pale, pale eyes, he looked suddenly human. Vulnerable. 'No,' he said, his voice like a growl in his throat. 'They're for living too.'

Esmé felt a surge of pity for him and was surprised by a sudden impulse to reach out and touch his hair. Her hand moved toward him before she even realized it and she made a fist and drew it back against her side. She was overcome by a powerful feeling of vertigo, as if she were standing at the edge of that crypt and it was deep, so deep, filled with rising mists of memory, with sulfur and scurrying things, and with terrible, terrible secrets. She had to steady herself against the wall, feeling silver and stone beneath her fingertips, and the old crust of liquified eyes.

Mihai watched her, and there was a look of longing on his face that sent a chill down her spine. She knew she'd seen it before, that same look, those eyes. And she remembered, again, the shock of his lips on hers.

But *how*? No man's lips, mortal or immortal, had come anywhere near her in her young life.

There came a thud against the door, harsh enough to vibrate through the entire chamber. Esmé gasped. Beasts were at the door. Since there was no bridge, they must have scaled the stalk of the spire itself. Their pounding jarred the silver eyelid and it slipped closed on its tiny hinges with a barely audible *tink*. The vision of the desert faded. A horrible moaning and wailing joined the pounding outside, and Esmé's heart began to race. Urgently she said to Mihai, 'Why did you bring me here? Take me home. Please!'

'Soon, Esmé,' he said.

'Soon? But they'll get in!'

'They won't. We're safe here.'

'Safe?' Esmé repeated with a hysterical laugh. And though she was afraid to know the answer, she cried, 'What do you want from me?'

'It's not from you, Esmé,' he said. 'Not really.'

'What—?' Esmé started to ask, but she caught sight of something then that made her freeze. As the last ghostly traces of the desert vision vanished from the mirror, she glimpsed a face in it. It was sunk in shadow, staring out, and it wasn't a vision. It was a reflection. There was someone right behind her. With a gasp, Esmé spun around.

In a darkened niche opposite the mirror sat a woman, still as stone. Dust was thick on her black hair and her shoulders, and it filled the lap of her silken robes. Her face was magnificent, a perfect golden oval, and her eyes were Druj blue. Dust clung to her lashes and one long strand of cobweb anchored there and spun away into the shadows. Her eyes were open but they were dry and dull and no life flickered in them.

'Who is that?' Esmé whispered, unable to look away from the woman's exquisite face.

'She is the Druj Queen.'

'Is she . . . is she dead?' asked Esmé, finding herself drawn closer to the shadowed Queen, taking tiny, cautious steps.

'Not dead. She is only empty. She left her body a long time ago.' He paused, then added, with a quick glance at Esmé, 'Fourteen years ago.'

'Fourteen?' Esmé repeated, turning to look at him as the significance of the number penetrated her awe. 'Fourteen?' she said again. Then she faced the Queen and admitted to herself what her first thought had been the instant she'd glimpsed that perfect face. The spark of recognition had been so subtle and yet so profound.

This beautiful creature looked nothing like her, but still, somehow, looking at her was like looking in a mirror.

· T E N ·

Yazad

G o to Yazad, Mab,' Mihai had said, and so when she was able to pick herself up off the floor, she did.

She stood beneath the elaborate arched gates of the old man's mansion and remembered the first time she had stood here – or, more accurately, *cowered* here in Mihai's arms. He had carried her through a window in the air from Tajbel straight to this spot, and it had seemed to her that the world had cracked open like an egg. The broad black avenue, the streetlamps and distant shimmer of city lights, the passing cars, the fumes – it had been, all of it, beyond her ken. It had been a terror.

She thought now that she must have seemed like some kind of creature to Yazad that evening, a quivering animal-girl at his door. She had held her belly in both arms, so full with Esmé she might have given birth at any moment, and he had looked at her with such compassion that her terror had eased a fraction. Never, never had she seen such a look. He'd guided her gently inside to a chair by the fire – another new and terrifying thing, fire! She'd thought it was a thing alive, that leaping flame. Yazad had given her tea, and then spoken long with Mihai in a language she couldn't understand.

There was so much in those days she couldn't understand, so much she still did not understand. Why had Mihai stolen her from the Queen? He had been devoted to her, and not in the same servile way as all the other Druj. From the moment Mab first glimpsed his face in the crowd, she had known he was different from the others. In the months he had been in Tajbel – all the months Esmé had been growing inside her – she had seen more baffling things than pain on his face. She had seen . . . *love*.

Her final night in Tajbel remained as much a mystery to her today as it had been then. It had been a full moon. The Druj were ritualistic in their moon worship and full-moon nights were always a celebration, a madness of fur and feathers and animal voices as they drew down their power from the luminous orb. On that night, as on any full moon, they had stripped off their robes and whispered themselves into animal cithrim one by one. The Naxturu howled. The winged ones whirled in the sky, screeching. The Queen stood atop her tower, changeless as always, watching them.

Mab remembered hoping her baby would come during the festival of the moon so that the Queen would be distracted, and she might keep the moment for herself. It was a small thing to hope for and the last hope she had, and she didn't have any notion then of it being a stupid wish. She'd seen cats birth their litters and she thought it would be like that for her too, silent and strained and miraculous, like good hard work. She hadn't understood what the pain would be like, so she had hoped her last hope, stroking her swollen belly and quietly whispering through her skin, 'Come out, bakham, my little gift, come out to me now,' while out in the night the Druj barked their mad moon songs.

But Esmé had not come. She'd kicked and swum within her and then settled down. Sometime in the night Mihai had appeared in Mab's doorway, making her jump. He only stared at her for a time before disappearing again as silently as he'd come, but Mab was unsettled by the look. She'd wondered why he hadn't shifted cithra like the rest of the Druj. He wasn't like the rest; she knew that, but she didn't know how.

He'd been in Tajbel for some time by then. It had been almost a year since Mab had focused on his face in that crowd of Druj, wondering at his suppressed grimace of pain while the Queen wore her body against Arkady for the first time. They'd taken Arkady away months ago, as soon as she missed her monthly bleeding. She'd cried for him at first, and for herself, to be alone again among the Druj, but then her belly had begun to grow, to *move*, and she realized she wasn't alone.

She had something to protect.

She thought of the endlessness of the mountains as she had glimpsed them long ago and escape had seemed as impossible as ever. But now she knew something she hadn't then: Out there, somewhere, were others. Like Arkady, like her. And so she had tried to escape through the woods for the first time, throwing cats to the beasts of her own free will, so she could flee across the bridge. Erezav and Isvant had found her so easily they'd barely even been angry with her. As they brought her back, handling her as carefully as if she were an egg – an egg containing their Queen's next pet – Mab realized they'd done this before, perhaps many times. They'd hunted down girl-mothers and brought them back. She wondered if her own mother had tried to flee. Yes, she thought. They all had. Of course they had.

And she tried again. And again. And again.

In the end, in a fury, the Queen had stood with her in the vestibule of her spire and whispered in a fierce rasp, *'Cinvat ni janat!'*

and knocked the bridge down, making Mab a prisoner in that lonely tooth of rock. The Druj could glide across the gap to the next spire, but she couldn't. She remembered the way the misery had welled up in her as she stood there, her arm gripped tight in the Queen's long fingers, looking out across the blackness of the chasm with no way to escape. The wind had picked up and the little cage had groaned on its iron rings as if to remind her it remained and would be used again after she was gone.

Hope had dwindled until all that remained was the wish to hold her child in her arms before they did to her whatever it was they did to spent pets.

But miraculously, it hadn't come to that.

Mihai came to her a second time that full-moon night, and this time he brought the Queen with him. There was feverish high color in both their faces and Mab had skittered into a nook in the rock wall of her room. She wept. She pleaded with them to leave her alone. But they had taken hold of her arms and eased her out of the nook in the wall. And as she had done so many times before, the Queen had slid her fingers under Mab's chin and tilted up her face. Mab saw her cast one questioning glance at Mihai, who nodded. 'You'll understand everything,' he said, and the Queen turned back to Mab. Through tears Mab looked into those hated blue eyes. The cold filled her.

And this time, oblivion came with it. She didn't remember anything after that until Mihai gathered her into his arms and carried her through a window of air, to London. To Yazad.

Now, Mab lifted Yazad's heavy door knocker and let it fall. The sound was like the crack of a gunshot. She lifted and dropped it again, and after a moment Yazad himself came to the door, not the butler Mab had been expecting. 'My dear,' he said, a warm smile lighting up his face. 'It's been too long.' He took her hand and pressed it between his. He knew it was the only touch she allowed. 'Come in,' he said, drawing aside to let her pass.

Mab stepped into the magnificent marble hall with its dripping shimmer of chandeliers and filigree of polished gold, remembering her first sight of it all and caring for none of it now. She looked at Yazad.

He was an old man, white-haired and brown-skinned, with wrinkles like the creases that deepen in fine leather over ages. His eyes were bright as a bird's, and they were brown, like her own. Yazad was human.

'Why did he take her?' she demanded.

'Come to the library, my dear,' he said. 'We'll talk there.'

She followed him. They walked over lush carpets in all the jewel colors of the Orient, past many-armed statues, bronze helmets, crossed scimitars, and almond-eyed madonnas glimmering with gold leaf. Yazad's home was a treasury of ancient beauties and the library was the most marvelous room of all. Mab stood in the doorway, remembering the way she had learned to read here with tiny Esmé cradled in one arm. Standing here in the house where Esmé had been born, Mab could almost *feel* her tiny daughter in her arms. Her arms and breasts would never lose their mute memories of holding that small body; they ached now with miserable yearning, and Mab let out a moan. 'Yazad,' she pleaded. 'What's happening to her? Do you know?'

'I do know, and I promise you Mihai will take care of her. He'll bring her back. Tea, my dear?'

'What? No! *When* will he bring her back? What's he *doing*?'

Yazad poured two cups of tea from a samovar anyway and set them out on a marble-topped table. 'He isn't doing anything,' he said with a sympathetic smile. 'He's only waiting now. What was done was done long ago, and it will be over soon. You can trust me when I tell you I know what Esmé is going through, Mab. I went through it myself when I was her age.'

'Went through *what*?'

'It was a different time, of course, a different land. A sudden blue eye did not go over well in the Srinagar of my youth!' He chuckled. 'The priests guessed I was possessed by a demon, but there were so many demons to choose from! They nearly killed me trying to cast it out. What terrible days those were!'

Mab stared at him. He was smiling and chuckling as he recounted his memories, and only the slightest flicker of uneasiness in his eyes hinted at their true unpleasantness.

'It was worse for me than for Esmé,' he went on. 'Much worse. You see, I was the first.'

'First *what*?'

'There was no word for it then,' he said. 'It was an accident, an act of despair that brought . . . unexpected results. Later, much later, Mihai started calling it *hathra. Wholeness*. I think it's a fine word.'

'Yazad!' Mab cried in exasperation. 'What's he done to her? You said your priests guessed you were possessed by a demon. But you weren't,' she said fervently, as if by declaring it she could make it so. 'You weren't!'

'No, my dear. I would say I was not *possessed* by a demon.' He paused, looking at her queerly, and Mab did not like the pause. He continued, 'Rather, I was . . . *incubating* one.'

'*Incubating?*' she repeated faintly.

'There's something *unsavory* about the word, I know, but I really think that's the best way to describe hathra. I was incubating a demon, but it hatched and no harm came to me, as you see. And no harm will come to Esmé, my dear. Mihai knows what he's doing far better now than he did in my time.'

'He . . . he . . .' Mab stammered, feeling herself once again on the edge of hysteria. 'He grew a demon in you?' she asked, her voice thick with outrage and disgust.

Yazad tilted his head to one side and lifted his heavy white brows. 'What? My dear, no. You don't understand. Mihai *was* the demon. He grew *himself* in me.'

'What?' Mab looked at him, bewildered. She shook her head. 'No, Yazad. That's not what this is. I've had Druj in me.' She shuddered. 'Hundreds of times! My eyes never turned blue. Neither did Arkady's when they went into him. This is something else.'

Yazad nodded patiently. 'Yes, it is. It's something else. Something marvelous. It's hathra.'

· E L E V E N ·

Hathra

In Tajbel's Tabernacle of Spies, Mihai tenderly brushed the dust of fourteen years from the Queen's hair and from her smooth cheeks. He blew lightly on her eyelashes to dislodge the cobwebs that clung there. Her dry, vacant eyes didn't even blink.

He turned back to Esmé, who was still staring at the Queen. 'I feel like I've seen her before,' she whispered. She shifted her eyes to Mihai and added, 'And you too. But I haven't. I remember things, but they're not my own memories. I know they're not.'

'What do you remember, Esmé?' asked Mihai.

'What? I don't know—' She glanced quickly at Mihai's lips and blushed and looked away.

He saw, and smiled. 'You remember kissing me,' he said softly.

'I've never kissed anyone!' Esmé protested.

'But you remember it, don't you?' He took a step toward her. The years of waiting had coiled him tight as a spring. He wanted badly to whisper himself into a wolf and run fast and far and let all the tension flood out of his underused muscles. He wanted to howl. But more than anything just now he wanted to hear this memory from Esmé's lips. 'Tell me,' he urged her.

Her eyes went vague as if she were slipping back inside the memory. Mihai leaned forward and listened. 'You'd been swimming,' she said to him. 'You tasted like river. Your hair was wet. It was winter, and blue slabs of ice came downstream like little ships. The melt had begun. You could hear it, the sluice and drip all down the mountain. Everything was still white, but it wouldn't be for much longer. It was cold. But . . . but your lips were warm.' Esmé's eyes refocused at once and her brow furrowed with confusion. She shook her head. 'It wasn't me,' she said warily, taking a step away from him.

'No, Esmé, it wasn't you.'

'Then why – ? What's happening to me?' Her young face was vivid with fear and she whimpered like a small animal. 'I remember other things too,' she whispered. 'Awful things.'

Mihai spoke very soothingly. 'It would be best if you could leave your mind clear now, Esmé. Listen to me. Think of a long corridor with doors on both sides. I want you to leave all the doors open. Okay? Just think of that corridor of open doors, and if you can keep your mind like that, it won't hurt very much.'

'It's going to hurt?' Esmé asked in a tiny voice.

'Not very much, my pretty pearl,' he murmured. 'Only a little bit.' He was lying. It would hurt. Like roots being ripped asunder, it would hurt. He was sorry for it, but he didn't know any other way.

It was the only way. He had discovered it by accident long ago.

Mihai came from a Druj citadel called Herezayen in the Tien Shan Mountains. It was a world of snowdrifts and ice, spruce forests without end, frigid lakes cupped in ancient rock. A world of wolf-song and wind. The Kyrgyz nomads called the land 'the mountains of the spirits,' and kept their yurts and goats on the lower slopes, well clear of the Druj who haunted the high places. Not that that kept them safe.

Life in Herezayen was a brutality of numbness. Time dripped

off the tips of icicles and Mihai's tribe did what they could to relieve the bleakness of their endless days. They hunted as they pleased, as wolves or eagles or snow leopards. They spied on humans when they could find them, and slipped inside of them too, though it was seldom rewarding. There was little fun to be had wearing the body of a lonely shepherd or a blunt-bodied woman who spoke a language of grunts and smelled of rancid grease. When they found human children wandering alone, they took them back to their cold caves and kept them. They tried to make them laugh, but the children were dull-witted and weepy, and such amusement as that provided grew wearisome very quickly.

Rarely, once every few decades, the dullness was relieved by a visit from the Queen. Mazishta, she was called, the greatest of them. She came in her sledge with her coterie of wolves and she expected them to drop to their knees and worship her. They did. Back at the fringes of their pale memories they could recall what had happened when some of their number had refused. Until the tides of oblivion crept up to swallow that gruesome day, they wouldn't fail in their worship, but they wouldn't be pleased about it either.

There was no love lost between tribes. Undoubtedly the Druj had all begun as one people, but long isolation had made them rivals. None of the far-flung Druj were pleased to greet the Queen and feel the lash of her power as she lorded her supremacy over them. The Herezayen Naxturu – including Mihai – and the Tajbel Naxturu had circled one another like warring wolf packs, their bloodlust only held in check by their Queen's indomitable will. If she had not been there, they would have torn one another apart. As it was, the Druj ranks were only waiting for the day her power would weaken and they could humble her – and her pack – as she had ever humbled them.

Still, as much as they resented her dominance, her visits and the raw pulse of her power did serve to remind them how their own power had fallen into disuse. It revived them for a time, but the revival never lasted long after she left. There seemed no escape from the desolation of life.

Mihai believed things had been different once. After all, someone had carved the magical symbols on the rock surfaces of Herezayen, and someone had written the books that had moldered in snow-drifts until no more words were legible. His mind ached to know what they had said, but the words were only smears now. And he didn't believe some forgotten ancestors had written them either – there *were* no ancestors. There were only themselves, their own interminable lives stretching from the lost beginning to the unknowable end. He himself might have written those books, but he had no memory of it.

He couldn't remember anything but the rhythm of monotony. When he tried to think of a time before, his mind became lost in a fog.

The day he left Herezayen, he went without forethought. He just started walking one day and kept walking. Thinking back, he realized there must have been a part of him that planned not to return or he'd have shifted cithra and flown that day as an eagle or leapt through the snow on broad, furred wolf paws, knowing that someone, upon his return, would whisper him back. But he hadn't shifted. He had struggled on in human form and gone further down the mountain, wending wide round wisps of hearth fires from the black, huddled yurts of the nomads. He hadn't turned back. He hadn't ever returned to Herezayen, and he hadn't shifted cithra since.

That was hundreds of years ago.

He drifted into the human world, across farms and into foul-smelling cities where they didn't know to fear him. He moved among them like a phantom, finding those humans who drew him in, some trick of their bright eyes beckoning to him like portals. Human eyes were like windows left open in a storm and it was a small matter to slip inside and mess about. He wore men and women both, and he danced in their feet, tasted with their mouths, and fought with their fists. He rutted in a haystack, one of their bodies pressed against another, and he passed himself back and forth between their moonlit eyes.

It was, all of it, a curiosity. The thrum of their blood enclosed him like a cocoon and it woke something in him, an almost-memory. But memory danced in the mists, taunting him, and never drew close enough to grasp.

He kept on because there was nothing else to do. He learned to leave his body and hunt over distances as an invisible animus searching for a host, so that his inert body might wait somewhere safe until he returned to claim it. He tried on warlords and priests and serving girls. He smelled the Black Death and nudged bodies out of his way with his boot. He fired an arquebus in the Battle of Pavia and shot the French king's horse out from under him. He started a mutiny on a slave ship. He mixed pigments for a Florentine master and tasted the carmine of crushed beetles on the tip of a sable brush.

He learned what quickens human hearts, how the touch of lips could make two lovers slip into a niche between moments so time rushes past them. He learned that a kiss could bring his almost-memories closer than anything else, but still not close enough to catch. It was sweet and bitter and maddening.

He broke the Druj taboos, all but one. He never destroyed a human soul, even in those days before he understood what they were, and now he was sick with relief for it. He ignored the taboo about entering children, though he used them lightly, and he entered an old woman once too, but only once, and learned there was a good reason for the taboo against the old. Her soul didn't slip aside for him; it filled her firmly and fully and left little room for his animus and for a startled, struggling moment he didn't know if *he* would escape. The old woman spit on the ground after he tore himself out of her, and he left the old alone after that.

He even braved fire – the only thing Druj truly feared – and was burned as a witch in a young woman's body. He wrapped her mind in a memory of flying as the flames took her and she felt no pain but smiled and spread her arms like wings. He felt it all, every flame, but it only burned her human shell and his animus surged out through her eyes with the departure of her soul. After that, haunted by the smell of her burning flesh, he lived in the Inquisitor for weeks and drove him mad, until finally his own lieutenants turned on him and clamped him in manacles still crusted with the blood of his victims. Mihai didn't undergo that bonfire. He let the Inquisitor suffer the flames all for himself.

Children, the old, fire – all the taboos broken but one. It was the final one that taught him what no other Druj knew, what he would later name *hathra*, and which would change his life forever.

When he'd seen a pair of bright black eyes peering from the shade of a chinar tree in high Kashmir, he had gone to the woman at once, drawn by something he couldn't divine, some mystery that suffused her like a light. Once he was inside of her, he knew at once what the mystery was. In the throb of her blood there was a second heartbeat, very fast – a life within, like a pearl enclosed. He had felt it before when trespassing into other women and he'd always obeyed the taboo. He had never touched an unborn life. But this time, without thought, he sank down into it with a kind of sigh.

To his surprise, he felt a calming darkness take him. And then there was nothing.

For years.

In the small dim chamber in Tajbel the beasts were still battering at the door, but Esmé seemed to have forgotten them. She was staring at her hands, turning them over, waving her fingers slowly like underwater weeds. She looked up anxiously at Mihai. 'I don't think these are my hands,' she whispered to him with a ragged intake of breath, holding them up to show him.

And as he looked at her, the brown iris of Esmé's right eye shimmered and began to fade, glinting in the gloom as it paled to Druj blue, just like her other eye. Mihai exhaled slowly and realized his own hands were shaking. 'My Queen,' he said, staring at Esmé, his voice heavy with emotion. 'I've been waiting for you.'

Esmé slowly blinked her twin blue eyes and stared back. 'Mihai . . .' she purred in a voice that did not belong to her. Then she gasped as she caught sight of the Queen on her throne behind him. She stared at her, then down at her own hands, then at the Queen again. 'What have you done to me?' she asked.

With a quaver in his voice he said, 'Fourteen years ago I told you you would understand everything, and you will. There are secrets, Sraeshta, about the Druj, so many things we've forgotten. We were not always thus, my Queen.' He paused, reached out, and grasped Esmé's fingers in his. 'I remember now. Once, a long, long time ago, we were *human*.'

Hatchling

Human. But that was long ago, in the years that humans now counted backward from the birth of the Nazarene. Then, Mihai had not been a demon; he had not always *been.* In that other time, there was a beginning. Mihai had been born human.

He only knew this because in 1564 he became human again for a short time.

He was a boy in Srinagar who poled boats in the shallows of Dal Lake and could skip stones better than any of the other boys. He worked in the orchards, tugging ropes tied to the peaks of the trees to dislodge any greedy birds that tried to steal the prince's cherries. If he pulled just right and released quickly, he could launch a thieving crow skyward like a stone from a slingshot. He was master of the wheeling bird shadows, little brown raja of the orchard. His name was Yazad and he prayed to an elephant-headed god and ate bread with poppy seeds and sesame. The sun warmed his skin, the breeze stirred his hair, and the soul within him felt as real as his heartbeat.

He didn't know anything else but being Yazad. Until the day his eye turned blue he didn't remember what he had been before, but the sight of that pale eye brought it all back, not at once, but in quickening surges. Memories battered him like ugly moths. He was besieged by them, and after a terrible struggle, days of madness and priests, his animus was shunted out into the air and his brief humanity came to an end.

He remembered the horror of finding himself unskinned, ripped from Yazad's soul and looking down from above at the boy whom he had thought was *himself,* seeing agony on that familiar face and trying to fathom that he was *not* Yazad, but only something that had been growing inside the boy like a parasite.

Bitterly, he knew himself again: Mihai, Druj, Naxturu. *Demon.*

He was just an invisible animus, adrift far from its abandoned body, bereft of the soul he had believed was his.

He had felt souls before within the bodies he had worn, but they were poor quivering things, thrust askew by his animus with as little care as robes hanging from a hook. This had been something else. Yazad's soul had been *his,* and he had been inside of *it* and it had been inside of *him.* Fear and pride and shame and fury and woe and *love* had moved through it and him like the shivers of harp strings. Every day had been a dazzle of sensation.

And now that soul was gone. It was like dying, but without the consolation of oblivion.

He let the distant, insistent tug of his body call his animus back across mountains from the green vale of Kashmir to the wilds of barren Persia. Years earlier he had left his body in an ancient tin mine of the Sassanid kings and it was still there. He flowed back into it and dusted it off, feeling his immortal shell with its pale eyes and wolfish teeth to be a cold home after his brief human life.

And if that cold life had been desolate before Yazad, it became nearly unendurable after. Mihai tried to return to his old ways. He happened upon a wedding and passed himself into the groom almost without thinking, but the feel of shoving into that young man's soul sickened him, like crushing a creature beneath his boot heel, and he'd withdrawn at once. He'd watched the wedding from a distance and wondered at the feeling of revulsion that had come over him.

He realized it was remorse.

Druj don't feel remorse.

Mihai began to understand that he was changed.

'Is that all souls are for?' Esmé had asked him earlier. 'For when we die?' Mihai could have laughed or cried when she'd asked him that. In all its simplicity her question was like cupped hands holding the meaning of his life.

'No,' he'd said. 'They're for living too.'

And because of Yazad, he had one. If not an entire soul, a shred of one. And Yazad had gotten something from him too. He had been born in 1564, after all, the year Michelangelo died and Shakespeare and Galileo were born, when people still believed the earth was the center of the universe. More than four hundred years had passed since then, and Yazad was still alive.

Such longevity was a mixed blessing, they would discover together.

Wearing his own body again, Mihai had traveled back to Kashmir and found the boy whose soul he had lived inside of. Seeing him again had been like getting back a piece of himself, and for Yazad it was the same. They were kin now, more than kin; they had been one creature, and together they felt something like wholeness.

Hathra.

They had traveled together after that, in and out of the centuries. Yazad had prospered. With the help of Mihai's magic he had become not only rich, but learned. He had collected artifacts and lore, learned the herbal cures the Druj used on human pets and beasts, even learned some animal language, and he had amassed a fortune in gold. At one hundred and fifty years old and still a young man, he had married a Mughal princess. Her father had objected and imprisoned her in the palace, but Mihai had sent a pair of giant ghorpad lizards up the sheer wall to carry her down and the three of them had escaped together across the desert. Tranquil Sahar had borne Yazad sons and daughters and they had all of them faded and died before even a hair of Yazad's own mustache went gray. Thus had he tasted the bitter residue of long life – to outlive all love.

When Mihai began to think of finding a new unborn soul to twin with, Yazad would only agree to help him on one condition: that any new host would never know his own loss and loneliness. If there was a solution, it was only to be found in magic, and so the two of them had bent themselves to it. They gathered books from forgotten places, but there was nothing written anywhere to help them. They experimented on their own with the language of the Druj. They had time, and in time, they wove the spell they wanted.

Over the next centuries, Mihai repeated his incubation a dozen times. He slipped into a dozen more human hosts, entering through a mother's eyes and slipping down into the kernel of incipient life within her, only to hatch years later with another shred of humanity to add to the patchwork soul he was making himself. Each time, his humanity deepened and something else happened. The mists began to clear. The almost-memories danced near like butterflies and he learned to cultivate stillness so they would alight upon him. And he began to remember.

And what he remembered pulled his world apart and rewove it in a new shape.

'We were human,' he repeated, still holding Esmé's hands, looking into her eyes and seeing only the Queen's eyes. Esmé was there too, a part of this now forever, but it was the Queen to whom he spoke. 'We had souls. We gave them up, Sraeshta. We were given a choice and we chose immortality.'

Esmé stared at him. She, or the Queen – for the moment there was no distinction – said faintly, skeptically, *'No.'*

'Yes. We didn't know what we would lose. We were so filled with our own power we didn't think that even the archangels could humble us! The things we had discovered had lifted us above the rest of humanity. We could change our shapes, become invisible, become weightless. We had mastered the elements. We rendered iron into gold, and rock into iron, and earth into water. We could send sickness on the air, and we sent the ill wind that slew the accursed Alexander who destroyed Persepolis and burnt Zarathustra's scriptures. We are great, Mazishta, and we are ancient, but back in the mists there is a time that we were children, you and I.'

And, he thought but did not say, a time that we *bore* children.

Esmé was trembling now, and despite the chill in the dank tabernacle, moisture had sprung up on her brow. Mihai reached out carefully to touch her and felt the heat radiating from her even before his fingers reached her skin. He knew what was happening. He'd been inside of it a dozen times but had never watched it from without. He thought watching would be harder to endure than the pain.

Esmé's soul and the Queen's animus had twinned and intertwined for fourteen years, and now they would be ripped apart. Like birth, this hatching came in its due course and nothing would stop it. He had hoped to tell his Queen more of their story first. Afterward, things would be . . . *difficult*. She would be herself again, more powerful than he by far, and she would see what he had done. How he had tricked her and stolen fourteen years, held her whole tribe prisoner in animal cithra while her spies' eyeballs rotted in their silver lids and her citadel fell to the beasts.

A beast roared and slammed at the door as if to punctuate Mihai's thought. The whole spire trembled and Mihai trembled too. He was afraid. His patchwork soul made fear a real and vivid thing and he loved even the fear, for he still remembered the numb absence of it. If he had the choice to make again, his soul for immortality, he knew what he would choose. But he wouldn't have that choice to make again. There was only one way that his benighted race might blend itself back into humanity – this secret way that he had discovered.

There was more he had hoped to tell the Queen before her animus hatched from Esmé's soul – so much more – but now was not the time. Esmé's blue eyes were glazing over. The pain was already taking her away. Yet there was one thing Mihai thought he could tell her now that might help. Taking Esmé's chin in his hand, he said, 'Mazishta, listen to me. Your true name, when you were human, it was Mahzarin. Golden moon. My beautiful Mahzarin.'

Esmé's eyes flared open and fluttered as memories unfurled within her. A sob broke from her lips. The beasts wailed outside the door. And pain descended like nightfall.

THIRTEEN

Almost-Memory

She had forgotten her name a long time ago. The mists had taken it.

But her name was Esmé. She was a girl with long, long, red, red hair. Her mother braided it. The flower shop boy stood behind her and held it in his hand. Her mother cut it off and hung it from a chandelier.

She was Queen. Mazishta. Her hair was black and her hand-maidens dressed it with pearls and silver pins.

Her flesh was golden like the desert.

Her flesh was pale like cream.

Her eyes were blue.

Brown.

She knew what it was like to hold eyeballs between her finger-tips. To toss cats to the beasts. To wrest babies from their mothers' arms. To kiss a fanged hunter in the snow. There was a crypt of memories at her feet, going deep into the earth. Things were starting to rise from it, on wings and tatters of mist. Things that horrified her.

Mahzarin.

She had forgotten her name.

She tried to hold her mind like a corridor of open doors, clear and ready for footfall, for whatever might dance past. Wolves, beasts, girl-mothers, stolen boys.

Rooftop dancing, a string purse filled with cherries and lace, fairy tale books embossed with gold.

And her body remembered things her mind did not. Whenever she had held the babies in the crook of her arm, she had been besieged with almost-memories, like fireflies never close enough to catch.

Mahzarin. She snatched the name from the air and held on to it as pain came down like drums and thunder and she felt herself begin to pull apart. She was a girl and she was a queen and back in the mists she was a woman who had seized the moon from the sky and drunk its light so that she would never die. And she never had.

The pain blinded her. It shattered the world into a maelstrom of jagged wings, beating and tearing at her. Falling to her knees, she imagined she was in a long corridor, and though she couldn't see or feel the doors, she tried to keep them open so the pain would find some egress after it had torn her in two.

· F O U R T E E N ·

The Kiss

Mihai held Esmé's head in his hands as she writhed on the floor of the tabernacle. Her screams had even shocked the beasts into silence, but after a moment they resumed their piteous moaning outside the door. Esmé's eyes were open, but Mihai knew she couldn't see anything but darkness and tangled memories. He cradled her head in his hands and her body between his knees to keep her from harming herself as she thrashed.

Seated in its niche, the Queen's body still did not stir, but soon it would. Mihai wished he could believe that his waiting was drawing to an end, but he was no fool. She might kill him for what he'd done, and he wouldn't even blame her for it. It would be a poetic end to his long, mad life, and sometimes death didn't sound bad at all, but simple and even a little sweet. Of course, he hoped for something else.

He had hoped for it since the day fifteen years ago when he had kissed his queen and everything had at last come clear.

It was luck or destiny that their paths had converged at all. Of all the places two bodies can be on a world, all the avenues and mine shafts and battlefields, they had found each other on the same desolate sweep of snow in mountains at the ragged fringe of Russia.

Mihai sometimes went away to bleak places when he needed an escape from the life he had chosen, with its welter of feelings and its dance of almost-memories opening themselves to him one by one. He had lived in thirteen human hosts and he knew hathra with them all, each one a part of him like blood in his veins. He laughed and wept with them and helped name their children, knew what they dreamed and helped them get it. And because of the magic he and Yazad had wrought, their long lives weren't spent alone. Their longevity, rather, proportioned itself amongst the ones they truly loved – soul mate, children – a measure of their years gifted to each, so that a beloved spouse might live long beside them, the span of years perhaps not as long as Yazad's, but richer.

Mihai had pieced together a soul of sorts, but he still didn't know what he *was*. The mists of memory were thin now, barely a veil, and there was something behind them always shifting, beckoning, receding. It exhausted him, straining to see through it.

He had been drawn to the Caucasus Mountains by some glimmer of instinct or impulse, and it had seemed an unreal coincidence when, after several days of quiet, he had heard wolfsong and known it was Druj. They were coming his way. He could have hidden himself, but he didn't. He waited, and soon the lunging black shapes shimmered out of the forest, and behind them glided the Queen's sledge, drawn by her enormous goats with their horns like swords.

In a matter of moments they were upon him, the wolves snarling, snapping. The Queen looked at him and his soul quailed. He had not seen her in hundreds of years, not since before he left Herezayen. Her beauty was seared into his memory; it was an unforgettable thing. But as he looked at her now, deeper, older visions stirred, remembrances that had been well lost in the mists when they had met in Herezayen.

She met his gaze, her pale eyes half-lidded with disinterest. To the wolves she said, 'Hunters, do you not know kin?' and they drew back, their snouts still furled with silent snarls. Her eyes did not flicker from Mihai's face. 'Is this not our naecish cousin from high Herezayen? The one who vanished?'

Mihai stiffened. *Naecish.* It meant *no one. Nothing.* It was what Druj called exiles. They had been known to kill exiles. The two largest wolves – Erezav and Isvant – were growling low in their throats and slavering, and Mihai thought they would be glad for the feel of his throat between their teeth. He looked back to the Queen and there was no sanctuary in her cold eyes. He could whisper himself into a falcon and try to escape, but if it came to that, he would likely wear those feathers forever; he had no one to whisper him back again. He could open a window in the air and flee through it, but they would follow. The Queen's power dwarfed his own; she could even whisper him dead if she chose.

He dropped to one knee and bowed his head. 'Mazishta,' he said. 'I didn't vanish. I went hunting a new quarry. I am no exile, but a wanderer in the mists.'

'The mists?' she said, not understanding.

'Those that veil our memories, Queen. It turns out that they are not . . . impenetrable.'

There was a flicker of interest and her eyes bored into him for a long moment. Mihai thought that she was mastering her desire to ask him what he meant, as if to show her curiosity would be to show weakness. She said only, 'Indeed,' in her purr of a voice.

He inclined his head slightly, never taking his eyes off hers.

There was movement from her sledge, and a whimper. The Queen's cold gaze flicked impatiently toward it and Mihai looked too. He saw a red-haired boy wrapped in furs, wrists and ankles bound, eyes immense with terror. The Queen's expression remained hard and cold and it sickened Mihai, all of it – the boy's terror and the Queen's calm – but he was careful not to show it.

'A boy, Mazishta?' he asked her, keeping his voice carefully careless.

'Yes.' She turned her attention back to Mihai and laid her fingers on a twist of red hair tied to the moonstone amulet around her neck. 'He wasn't easy to find. This red is a rare shade. Does it not look like blood in the moonlight?'

Mihai looked at the hair, not understanding. In the moonlight it did have the sheen and shade of blood. He nodded.

'My izha has grown up,' said the Queen with a hint of regret. 'They grow up so fast, humans.'

Izha. Milk sacrifice. Across the centuries Mihai recalled that the Queen had bred human pets in Tajbel. He kept his face still as stone and swallowed his disgust. 'More slowly than most creatures,' he said.

'I suppose that's true. What other creature is helpless for so many years?' she replied.

Mihai was watching her minutely or he might not have noticed the way her fingers fluttered slightly as her hands half lifted themselves to her belly. They dropped away again, but Mihai had seen. He knew the way his own body had held on to memories that the mists had conspired to erase, and the gesture she had unconsciously made – he had seen it before. For centuries, after all, he had hunted pregnant women and watched them, making his choice for his next host. Hers was a gesture of one who knew what it was to carry life inside.

It was impossible. Druj didn't quicken. The Queen could have no such memories.

Mihai struggled to keep his voice flat as he said, 'So the boy is for breeding.'

'Yes.'

Mihai looked at the miserable, terrified boy and forced himself to smile. 'Compliments. No doubt they will breed you a lovely pet.'

The wolf Isvant growled and Mihai could tell he wanted the Queen to whisper him back to his human cithra so that he could face Mihai eye to eye, but she didn't oblige him. She said to Mihai, 'Mist-wanderer, you have been too long absent from your own kind. You will return with us to Tajbel, and I will decide what is to be done with you.'

The thought of living again among Druj was abhorrent, but Mihai was in no position to refuse. He inclined his head.

She said, 'Come. We travel until sunrise. And when we stop, you can tell me something of the mists.'

'As you wish, Rathaeshtar,' he replied. She urged her goats on and the sledge gathered speed. The wolves bounded through the snow, and Mihai followed. The Queen looked back over her shoulder. 'Are you not Naxturu? Won't you shift cithra?' she asked.

'I keep this shape now.'

She didn't ask him why, but he saw that her eyes, which had been dull and hard when she had first come upon him, were aglitter now with savage curiosity. He knew she didn't shift either. There had long been murmurs in his own tribe that they didn't need a Queen, and Mihai guessed she didn't trust even her own Naxturu to whisper for her out of suspicion they might choose to leave her trapped in wolf form. She kept her flesh under her own command, as did he.

He ran behind the sledge, his gait long and easy, and they made their way higher into the mountains. They stopped at sunrise beside a river and the Queen gave the red-haired boy frigid water to drink and whispered her wolves back to human cithra. There were six of them, three males with the heavy hunched shoulders of Naxturu who spent as much time as wolves as they did as humans, and three females, slimmer but just as bestial as their male counterparts. They stretched their naked bodies in the falling snow and all but one chose to whisper themselves back to wolves and curl up to sleep through the day, dug into snow burrows. Only Isvant kept his human cithra. He sat naked with his back against a tree and glared at Mihai.

Mihai returned the look, but he kept his face impassive. It wasn't easy. It had been a very long time since he had been in the company of his own kind. He wondered if they would see the change in him somehow, or maybe smell it. He was sitting on a rock beside the river and suddenly he couldn't stand Isvant's scrutiny. He stood and stripped off his clothes and dove into the water. It was snow-melt cold and it served to shock him out of his uneasiness. He surfaced. The current was carrying him away; he swam against it with powerful, easy strokes. Isvant stood and watched to make sure he didn't try to escape. Mihai swam back to the bank, shook himself, and sat naked beside his clothes.

His hair was still streaming when the Queen joined him. She sat beside him on the rock. 'Tell me about the mists,' she said, her voice half-whisper, half-purr.

So, Mihai thought, her curiosity had gotten the better of her. Still staring ahead at the black water with its traffic of swift ice, he said, 'I used to think they were a boundary, an ending beyond which there was nothing. But what if they're not? What if the mists are like the edge of the map when the cartographer has drawn all he knows, when the explorers' ships have not yet delved the unknown? What if there's more?'

'More?'

'Surely you've felt it. When you go into a human, your almost-memories sharpen. Each time, you believe you will remember.'

She didn't respond at once and he didn't look at her. After a long pause she said, very quietly, 'Yes.'

'And it becomes a madness and a need, but you never remember.'

Again, 'Yes.'

'And you're certain that once there was something else. Your *body* remembers it.'

'Yes.' Her voice sounded raw now.

'The thing your body remembers most . . .' Mihai began, turning to glance at her. For the second time he glimpsed the subtle movement of her arms and hands. It was, unmistakably, the gesture of a woman who knows what it is to be full with child. His words faltered. Deep within himself, a memory shifted. Mists parted. Something drew into the light. His eyes flared wide when he saw what they were and the Queen saw his shock before he could hide it.

Her own eyes narrowed in suspicion, but there was something else in them too. A gleam of hunger.

'What?' she demanded. 'What does it remember most?'

Mihai's thoughts moiled and spun and he fought to hide his confusion, sure that any moment it would reveal his otherness and give her a reason to end his life. 'For me,' he said, with an effort at calmness, 'the thing that brings the memories closest is . . . a kiss.'

'A kiss!' she repeated, surprised.

It wasn't a lie. Something about a kiss, back when he had worn humans, had always fanned at the mists like a gusting wind, chasing them back, thinning them, to show him the shadows of what waited within. He chanced a look at the Queen. There was a small, quizzical smile on her perfect lips and he tried smiling too, though his heart was beating fast as a human's and memories were rising up around him like ghosts. With absolute clarity, he knew something he had never guessed. He had not felt such a deep shuddering shock since his animus was dragged out of Yazad's soul. That time, he had discovered he was not human. This time, he remembered that he had been.

'Mazishta,' he whispered. 'There *was* something else once, something more. I've seen it.'

Her smile faded and he could see her longing to believe him. 'What have you seen?' she asked in a husky whisper.

You, he wanted to say. I have seen *you*. But he said, 'I have seen a woman with a mind as sharp as a shard of obsidian, and as brilliant as the moon. Mysteries opened themselves up to her and revealed their quiet centers. She wanted to know everything. She wanted to live forever.'

'And?'

'And she did,' whispered Mihai. For a moment his careful mask slipped and he knew by her widening eyes that she had seen his real face, haunted and hungry and stricken by the sudden memory of something she couldn't fathom. *Love.* He expected her to draw away from him in disdain, but she didn't.

She kissed him.

She leaned into him, sinuous as a predator, and touched her lips to his and held them there in mimicry of kisses she had witnessed. There was nothing sensual in it, not at first, just the chaste press of skin. But then her lips parted ever so slightly and Mihai felt her tremble as, just for an instant, there passed a ghost of the way they had kissed in a long-ago life when they had loved each other, soul and skin, and slept entwined, sharing dreams through their flesh and waking in the dark to the slow pull of pleasure.

Before she had been the Queen of the Druj, she had been Mahzarin, and she had been his. Once upon a time, she had hooked her small foot around his leg and drawn him up against her. He had taken her earlobe between his teeth, tasted the hollow at the base of her throat, and sung through the skin of her taut belly while she grew his daughters within her. Her black hair had fallen across his pillow like a shadow every night and he had slept and woken upon it. He remembered how her flesh had felt when it was human and warm, and not immortal and icy.

But *she* would not remember it. And she would not believe it.

Her breath quavered, then her eyes flew open wide and she reeled away from the kiss. There was fascination and a hint of disbelief in her look. She stared at Mihai's lips. She lifted her fingers to them and hesitated, then touched them quickly as if they might burn her. 'Your . . . your lips are *warm*,' she stammered. *'How?'*

But Mihai didn't have a chance to answer her. He caught a flash of movement from the corner of his eye and looked just in time to see Isvant's body come hurtling at him, human as he left the ground, his flesh morphing to fur as he flew through the air. When he hit Mihai, he was wolf, claws slashing and fangs bared. The two toppled backward into the river and were lost under the black water.

Mihai's blood surfaced before he did.

H e lived. Druj are not so easy to kill. Only fire can accomplish it, or the severing of the head from the neck. Isvant did neither of these things; he only raked Mihai's chest from collarbone to navel and sank his fangs into the muscle of his shoulder. It was not pleasant, but it was no risk to Mihai's life. After he dragged himself out of the river, he whispered the wounds closed, left his blood on the snow, and got up to struggle back into his clothes.

The Queen came and stood before him for a brief moment and looked into his eyes. She was tall; they met eye to eye, and Mihai saw her hesitate before reaching out quickly to touch his lips once more. When she did, the troubled look went out of her eyes. His lips were as cold as the river, just as Druj flesh should be, and she turned on her heel and went to her sledge, pausing briefly to run her fingers through her human boy's red hair.

She didn't mention the kiss again or the memories it had unlocked – if, indeed, it had unlocked any. For Mihai it had. Watching her across the snow, he could picture her so clearly from many centuries past, balancing a black-haired baby girl on each hip. Arzu and Lilya, their twin daughters had been called. *Wish* and *Lily*. Mihai wanted to tell her that her body remembered the weight of her own flesh-and-blood children, but he wouldn't. She wasn't Mahzarin now. She was Queen of the Druj, only a soulless echo of the woman she had once been. In any case, he had no chance to tell her. She didn't come near him again.

They continued on to Tajbel and her sledge traveled fast through the snow, the wolves flanking her. Isvant doubled back and watched Mihai constantly, and Mihai watched him back. He knew the body could remember hate as it could remember the weight of a child or the pressure of a kiss, and Isvant had always hated him, even if the hunter didn't remember why. Mihai remembered why – Isvant had loved Mahzarin too, in the time before – and he didn't grudge him the hate.

But he did grudge him his brutal charade of intimacy with the Queen once they arrived in Tajbel.

He had to stand in the throng of Druj and watch as the red-haired boy and the Queen's izha were thrust toward each other, painted in their bizarre spirals of blue. Their terror was thick as musk, and Mihai thought that was part of what excited the Druj. But only part of it. Druj sense-memories were a kind of ineluctable torment, like an itch they could never scratch. It was an awful irony that the last vestiges of their humanity, the phantom memories contained in their skin, were what drove them to this grim violation.

But he understood. Wasn't that same torment what had driven *him* to wear human after human himself and, ultimately, to break the taboos?

At first, no coherent thought could break through his anguish and he spent all his energy concealing it as the humans were mated with each other like animals. He did a poor job, he thought, but fortunately no one was watching him, held in thrall as they were by their sick excitement. Only the girl herself seemed to fix on his face in the instant before the Queen tilted up her chin and took her over.

And Isvant took over the boy and grabbed the girl by the wrist.

Through all that followed, the Queen's body – Mahzarin's body – stood by empty as a statue, a vivid reminder to Mihai that although he had struggled his way back from his own execration, pieced together a makeshift soul from shreds, and found with a weary kind of amazement that he could *love*, it little mattered. The woman he loved was a monster. And she could never love him back.

'Naecish,' she said to him later. 'You'll stay in the Naxturu spire with the hunters where you belong.'

She meant it as an honor, he thought. He wouldn't be held prisoner here but would keep his caste status. It was unexpected, and the Naxturu wouldn't like it, and he didn't either. Mihai knew where he belonged, and it was not with the Naxturu. It was not with the Druj at all. 'Queen,' he said softly. 'I told you, I am a different kind of hunter now.'

'Ah, yes,' she said with a hint of disdain. 'A hunter of *mists*. Well, we have no caste of mist-hunters, have we? Perhaps the astronomers' tower would be more suitable.'

He was supposed to decline. The castes were fixed: Naxturu were Naxturu as wolves were wolves. Would a wolf suddenly take up residence with a nest of serpents or hawks? No; it was against nature. Nevertheless, Mihai said, 'It would be, Mazishta, I thank you.'

She showed no surprise, only stared at him a beat too long. 'Very well,' she said. 'Vanghav,' she called, summoning a Druj to her side. 'The naecish is to be your guest.'

Vanghav didn't question the decision, but Isvant did. 'Sraeshta,' he growled, coming up behind her. 'The exile should be in a cage.'

'*Tajbel* is a cage,' she said lightly, and Mihai had to agree. Though not as desolate as Herezayen, there was something awful about the Queen's citadel with its tusks of rock, its black chasm, and the beasts that lurked there. He'd glimpsed only their arms flashing up from beneath the bridges, but their stench was everywhere, and it was alien. He didn't know what the creatures were, but he was certain they existed nowhere else. Knowing the Queen's awful power, he thought she must have *made* them. But out of what? What had she transformed into these foul guardians of Tajbel? Some unfortunate humans, long ago? Druj who had displeased her? He shuddered at the thought.

'He could escape—' said Isvant, but the Queen cut him off.

'Don't worry. He'll be watched. Come with me,' she commanded, and they followed her down a curving stair to a doorway low on her spire. They stood at the threshold as she unlocked the door, and waited there when she entered. The room within was dark, but Mihai could make out the glint of silver and hear the quiet swivel of small hinges. Peering in, he saw eyes, dozens and hundreds, watching him from the shadows. At a glance they seemed to be a horde of creatures hunched in darkness, still as cats on the prowl. But he quickly saw there were no creatures – only disembodied eyes. It was his first sight of the Tabernacle of Spies.

The Queen brought a lizard out of the darkness. It was collared and chained to a manacle, and this manacle she put around Mihai's upper arm. It clicked shut and she set the lizard on his shoulder, from which perch it peered at him with a single golden eye. Its other was somewhere in the tabernacle behind one of the silver eyelids. 'For you,' said the Queen. 'A pet.'

'A *spy*,' he said.

'Yes, of course. But treat him as a pet. Feed him, *name* him if you like, and take care nothing happens to him. I'll be watching, naecish.'

He didn't name the lizard, not at first, but through the months of tolerating its golden-eyed scrutiny he grew rather fond of it and dubbed it Zaranya. *Golden*. Its weight on his shoulder, even its flicking tongue, made him feel less alone in the bleak austerity of Tajbel.

And he *was* alone. Even with a crush of Druj around him he felt that he and Zaranya were the sole living creatures in a city of the undead. Well, not the sole living creatures. There were the beasts, in their awful hunger more alive than the Druj, and there were the cats, and of course, there were the two young humans. Seeing them together only deepened Mihai's despair.

In the weeks that followed their first mating he watched them from the corner of his eye and, attuned to their humanity as the rest of the Druj were not, he saw what began to grow between them. Though the blue spirals were painted again and again and the Queen and Isvant repeated their charade almost daily, there were many more hours in which the young girl and boy were left alone. And how, in this place, could they fail to turn to each other for comfort?

One day several months in, Mihai saw them sitting side by side in the sun in the highest window of the Queen's spire, their thin legs hanging over the edge. He watched the way their shoulders touched, the shy way their eyes met, peering up through their lashes. How they hooked pinkies when they rose to their feet to go back inside, as if they were just children walking to a bus bench and not captives in a wilderness of demons.

Those hooked pinkies almost made him weep. He thought of Mahzarin as she once had been and, with a violence that made his soul shudder, he wished for an innocent touch like that. He even wished for a glance. Since their arrival in Tajbel she had scarcely looked at him. She had the business of ruling her citadel to see to, and she was much occupied with her two young humans, but whenever Mihai was near her, she seemed always to be looking elsewhere. He thought there was something a little too careful in her coldness, as if by avoiding him she was trying not to betray something inside herself, and he knew well what that was.

It was hunger. Once it had driven him too. The Queen tried to hide it, but she had a hunger for humanity, for warm flesh and quick blood and memories. She played it out in her izha's body, and she locked herself for hours in her tabernacle, watching lives unfold in distant lands through the eyes of her hundreds of spies. And through Zaranya's eyes, she watched Mihai. He might never have known how often she watched him, or how false her feigned indifference was, if not for Isvant.

'I'm going to kill him,' he heard the hunter say to Erezav. The two were three spires away in the Naxturu tower and Mihai shouldn't have been able to hear them so clearly, but he whispered to the breeze and it carried their words to his ears.

'She watches him,' Erezav replied. 'She'll know.'

'She can't watch him forever,' spat Isvant. Then in a sudden fury he snarled, 'What does she see, anyway? She watches the nae-cish as much as she watches the humans. Locked away with her mirror! What is there to see but an exile who should be fed to the beasts?'

'Or *become* a beast,' said Erezav.

Isvant gave a terrible kind of laugh. Druj did not often laugh; they did not know humor. This wasn't humor, but a curdled snarl of vengeance that came out as an awful chuckle. 'Yes,' he said. 'But only Mazishta has that power, and while he's her fascination she won't do it.'

'Her fascinations don't last,' said Erezav.

'No, they don't. But I don't want to wait until she's through with him. I'll kill him when she's not watching him—'

'She's always watching him.'

'Not always. Not on the full moon.'

The Queen presided over full moons on the platform atop her spire. She stood with her head thrown back and let the white light flood into her and charge her with its power. Mihai could remember now the first time she had drunk the moonlight, long, long ago. He'd been at her side and had seen her lit from within. It had been the beginning of everything. If only they had known then the price of their power.

Erezav said to Isvant, 'She'll notice if you don't shift.'

'She won't,' he said bitterly. 'She doesn't notice me at all.'

And so Mihai took care to guard his life, making certain Isvant could never surprise him, and a new layer of desperation was added to his existence in Tajbel. 'Her fascinations don't last,' Erezav had said. Mihai could well imagine they did not. He knew he couldn't stay here; if he did, things would not end well for him. Nor could he escape; there was nowhere in the world he could hide if the Queen chose to pursue him, and . . . he didn't wish to escape. Even in her soullessness, the sight of her face was like a conduit to his oldest memories: her skin, warm beneath his own. Her belly, magnificent with child. Their daughters, soft as velvet and dark-eyed as they too once had been.

Memories held him in limbo.

It wasn't until the Queen's izha became pregnant that Mihai acknowledged to himself the plan that had been growing in the shadows of his mind – the life within the red-haired girl, like a pearl enclosed. Thirteen times had he slid his own animus into the darkness of an unformed soul and concresced with it. But it was not his own animus he thought of when he looked at the smooth curve of the girl's swelling belly. It was the Queen's.

He was careful. He waited, and on a full moon late in the girl's pregnancy, when all the other Druj – including Isvant – had shifted into wolves and owls and stags, he went to the Queen.

'Mazishta,' he said. 'What if I told you I knew how you could go into the mists and capture the memories that dance away from you as you reach for them?'

Her eyes grew bright.

'The old god breathed the mist into our minds. It's meant to keep us blind, to keep us from learning what we were and finding our way back to it. There is a way, but it is barred by taboo.'

'Which taboo?' she demanded.

'The unborn,' Mihai said, and she understood at once, as he knew she would. It was so simple. Her hunger was so great it took no urging from him at all. Together they descended to the girl's chamber and went in to her. The boy had been taken away months ago and she was alone. She saw the excitement in their faces, and terror bloomed in hers. She clasped her hands over her belly and ducked her head, trying to hide her eyes from them, to close herself up tight like a flower bud.

But there was nothing she could do. The Queen tilted back her head by force and Mihai's heart ached to see the girl's terror.

'You'll understand everything,' he assured the Queen, and then, suddenly, it was done. Her perfect body stood vacant. Mihai waited for an agonized moment to see if she had done as he instructed. He watched the girl. Her eyelids fluttered and she looked up at him, bewildered. She had felt the Queen pass into her but instead of possessing her entirely, the cold had seemed to pour right through her. Before she could wonder where it had gone, Mihai whispered her to sleep, catching her body and cradling her for a moment in his arms, his hand splayed tenderly over her belly, before laying her down on her bed of furs.

He did not want her to suspect what she carried within her.

He took the Queen's body down to her Tabernacle of Spies, kissed her on the brow, his lips lingering against her icy flesh, and he left her there. He locked her in and tucked the key into his pocket. He broke the manacle that chained Zaranya to him and set the lizard free, almost sad to part company with it, and then he returned to the girl. It was still night when he took her away through the glimmering window to London and closed the air behind them, sealing Tajbel from their sight. The wolves still howled at the brilliant moon and the owls and ravens and hawks still spun in the sky, and their sounds choked off when the window closed.

When the dawn came in Tajbel, those Druj would go in search of the Queen to receive her whisper and be restored to their human cithrim, but they wouldn't find her. In the tabernacle her body was vacant, no animus for them to scent or trace. They would remain as beasts, their sharp teeth and beaks unable to speak the magic that was locked within them. Nor could they ever prostrate themselves before other tribes to beg their whispers; rivalries ran too deep. Their brother and sister Druj would be all too happy to see the Tajbel tribe powerless and without the protection of their Queen.

In London, Mihai felt no remorse. Better they be animals in the skins of animals, he thought, than in the guise of humans. He watched from the corner as Yazad comforted the pregnant girl with his soothing voice, saw how she cowered like a hunted creature, spooked by the firelight, overawed by everything. He remembered the twist of her hair on the chain of the Queen's amulet, and remembered the boy's hair, how he had been hunted down and captured because of it, and he felt nothing at all for the Druj in Tajbel.

He took one long look at the izha's full, ripe belly and imagined what silent weaving was at work within her, what fibers of soul and animus were even now growing together like roots interlocking in soil. He left through the window, leaving the girl in Yazad's care.

He had only to wait.

Those fourteen years were the longest of his very long life.

SIXTEEN

Ashes and Dust

Once, many centuries ago,' Mihai said in a low, strained voice, holding Esmé to his chest as she writhed and screamed, 'a sect of worshippers went in secret to the dakhma outside their city. It was not a place for the living. It was the high, lonely tower of silence where the dead were left so their putrefaction would corrupt neither sacred earth nor holy fire. It was a place of vultures and mysteries.

'The moon shone down on the raw bones of the dead and the worshippers decided they would never die. They were not simply worshippers, these black-haired men and women. They were sorcerers, theosophists, and scholars. Among them was a woman with a mind as sharp as a blade of obsidian, brilliant as the moon. Mysteries unfurled themselves for her like flowers and revealed to her their quiet centers. Secrets gathered for her out of the stars and she drew them down from the sky and shaped them into a new faith, gifting herself and her followers with power, and with immortality.

'But the old god would not have it. He snatched out their souls and laid them flat on a rock and he made them choose between what he had given them and what they had taken for themselves. The woman made the choice.

'She chose immortality and the others followed her. And so the god scorched their souls to ash and scattered them in the wind. He dubbed them Druj. *Demons.* He breathed a mist into their memories and he plucked their children from their arms to grow old and die as humans, and he flung the Druj to the mountains where they could begin their immortality in landscapes of desolation that reflected the emptiness within them. He told them they would be purged by fire at the end of time, when the whole world would be transfigured by light. If they could gather their scattered souls by then, he said, they would be transfigured too. If not, they would plunge forever into the abyss. And until they found their souls, fire, he said, which was sacred to him, would be anathema to them. Even ash would burn them.

'He told them all of this, but the mists ran rampant in their minds and they forgot everything, remembering only their fear of the holy fire and ash, but not the reason for it.

'They forgot their humanity and they forgot the children who had been wrested from their arms. They forgot the drifting ash of their souls that was as dust upon the skin of the world.

'The centuries passed. They lived and lived. They grew weary of immortality but remembered nothing else. And then one day, something happened that led one among them to discover all that had been forgotten.'

It had taken Mihai thirteen cycles of hathra, thirteen souls interknit with his animus, for the ashes of his soul to gather again inside of him, bringing his memories with them, piece by piece. His human hosts were more than family to him. They were a new tribe spread through the world, in London and Astrakhan and Jaffna and New York and elsewhere. And as was he, they were a new creation.

They would live for centuries and die as humans, souls intact, and so would Esmé.

As Mihai watched, her eyes began to change again. The pale blue turned cloudy and then darkened. She gave a convulsive shudder and a wrenching scream that wore on and on until her throat was raw, and then she lay still, her eyes open and glazed – and *brown*. Mihai stroked her cheek and whispered into her ear. Not magic whispers, not Druj words, but only an English lullaby.

And behind him, the Queen of the Druj slowly turned her head.

Mihai looked up at her. Their eyes met. 'Mihai,' she whispered.

'Mahzarin,' he said. 'My love.' His voice trembled.

A look of confusion swept over her face. Her gaze dropped to Esmé, still cradled in Mihai's arms. When she looked back up at Mihai, there was only bewilderment in her eyes.

Mihai rose to his knees and laid Esmé carefully on the floor. 'My Queen, I have much to tell you,' he said. He could hear the fear in his own voice.

She had always been a wild font of power, even back when she had been his wife and had borne Arzu and Lilya. There had never been a more powerful sorceress; without her, indeed, their immortality would never have been possible. There would never have been Druj. Mahzarin was the heresiarch who had unraveled the mysteries. She had created the new magic that had angered the old god. And, Mihai thought, she would eventually remember it. He feared she would have just enough humanity now to grieve for what she'd done – but not enough to love him.

The beasts had been silenced by Esmé's last terrible scream. Now, as Mahzarin stared at Mihai in confusion, one let out a long moan outside the door. Mahzarin rose to her feet in a fluid motion, as if she had not sat still for fourteen years. A great cloud of dust fanned from her silken robes and her black hair.

On the floor, Esmé tried to sit up.

Mihai looked from girl to woman. Two lovely, frightened faces, as different as night and day, gold and ivory, joined forever now, even if they didn't realize it yet. Esmé made a small sound like a kitten might make. Mihai was between them. His soul strained toward Mahzarin. He wanted only to drink in the sight of her, but he knelt and grasped Esmé in his arms and helped her to sit up.

Mahzarin saw the silver eyelids on the wall and she took in the rot. Beasts bellowed at the door and she swung toward it. Mihai saw that fury was building in her as her memories sifted themselves into a kind of order. Her lips went white. She swept past Mihai to the door. He held the key in his pocket but she didn't need it. With one whispered word she blew it off its hinges and it clattered down over the end of the broken bridge and into the chasm, taking beasts down with it. Their long, falling cries grew distant. Others still clung to the spire. Their arms flailed into the open doorway.

Mihai watched, awed. Esmé clenched her eyes shut and cowered against him. Mahzarin stood like a wrathful goddess and whispered another word, snarled it, and the beasts seemed to be torn off the spire by some huge invisible hand, plucked like spiders and dropped. They fell away into the blackness, wailing. Mahzarin went out onto the step and saw her devastated citadel spread before her. Beasts clung everywhere, starved and moaning, stone crumbling beneath their long white arms. Mahzarin's breath came fast. Her eyes took on the glassy sheen of fever. 'Mihai,' she growled, baring her fangs, and swung around to face him.

But he was gone and so was Esmé. In the shafts of light the dust of fourteen years was spinning from their departure. The tabernacle was empty.

The Queen of the Druj let out a terrible howl that echoed through Tajbel. Far off in the forest, some of her scattered animal subjects heard and rejoiced. On the cliff walls and the stone stalks of the spires, the beasts cowered. They remembered her, but dimly. Their hunger was stronger than their fear. They kept on coming. In a rage she faced them, and in her pain and confusion her power burst forth like a hurricane, sweeping away everything in its path.

SEVENTEEN

Waiting

A few weeks later, Mihai and Mab crossed paths in Yazad's library. She was coming out, he was going in, and he drew aside to let her pass, noticing with an ache of remorse how she didn't even seem to see him. She was like a sleepwalker these days, and the haunted look in her eyes reminded him of the child she had been in Tajbel when she was a pet without a name. 'I'm sorry,' he whispered to her back, but she didn't seem to hear.

He continued into the library, pulling Esmé's severed red braid out of his pocket. The girl was sitting in a deep chair by a window, staring out. Mihai uncoiled the braid and dangled it in her line of sight until she came back from whatever daydream or memory she had been wandering in and blinked. 'My hair,' she said sadly.

'It took you fourteen years to grow this,' he said. 'And you just left it hanging from a chandelier? Careless.'

'I'm not,' she protested. 'My mother—'

'I know. And if you turn around, I'll put it back.'

'Really?' she asked, looking up at him.

Mihai smiled and nodded. Esmé sat forward and turned her back to him. She heard him whisper, felt the gentlest stirring at the nape of her neck, and then, all at once, the weight of her hair was restored so her head tilted back with the suddenness of it, like a scale at the market when apples are dropped in. She reached back and there was her braid as if it had never been cut. 'I already forgot how heavy it is,' she said, unamazed by this small gift of magic.

She had recently been told she would live for hundreds of years. She would be difficult to amaze from now on.

She asked, 'Are you going to put my mother's back too?'

Mihai shook his head, letting his gaze drift out the window. 'She doesn't want me to touch her,' he said.

Esmé was quiet, watching him. She realized she still saw him through the Druj Queen's memories. She remembered the wintery kiss as if her own lips had touched his, and she remembered other things too, much less pleasant things, like the feeling of trespassing in her mother's soul. Yazad was going to help her misplace those memories. Hypnotism, he had said, holding up a crystal on a silver chain and smiling in the twinkling way he had that made everything seem like a grand adventure.

'Well, thanks,' she said, running her fingers down the braid that was now draped over her shoulder.

'You're welcome,' Mihai replied. He turned to go.

'Mihai?' Esmé asked.

'Yes?'

'All the other Druj with their souls scattered,' she said slowly. 'Will you . . . help them . . . too?'

'Help them? I don't know,' he said. The thought overwhelmed him. Among all the citadels there were hundreds of Druj. As for 'helping them,' he didn't see how he could. Mahzarin could, certainly, if she ever came to him and learned the ways of hathra. He couldn't think beyond that hope. Weeks had passed and now the fear of what she might do to him had subsided entirely and been replaced by the fear that she would do *nothing*, that she would rebuild Tajbel and remain there, ignoring the humanity that he had given her. That *Esmé* had given her. Esmé was waiting for her too. Hathra was a strange thing; she might hate the Druj Queen who had done such terrible things to her mother, but she still felt her absence like a rift in her soul.

Mihai touched Esmé lightly on the top of her head and walked out. He left Yazad's and wandered through the city, smelling the density of humans all around him, feeling their jostling shoulders in the crowds. When he felt saturated with humanity, he scaled lizard-like the side of a church and perched on the spire so the sky lay open all around him.

And he went on with his waiting.

Mab and Esmé returned to their flat and to their pretty little lives, though of course, things would never be the same for them. Mab watched her beloved daughter warily now, as if she didn't really know her. The thought that all along, while she had believed them safe, Esmé had carried Mab's tormentor within herself . . . it was a shock that would not easily fade. It was all the horrors of her youth unveiled anew, compounded by betrayal. That betrayal and shock became the backdrop and stage dressing of her mind; any other thought she might have was as a transient actor treading past. Always, the betrayal was there behind it. Always, after any other thought, her mind reverted to it, and it had the power to leave her breathless and gasping in an instant, like a punch to the gut.

Yazad had explained that Esmé and the Druj Queen were con-nected now by a bond Mab would never understand, a bond that would live on long after she herself was dead. Her daughter and her enemy shared a soul, and some day, Yazad warned her, Mahzarin would come. Mab leapt at every sound, scarcely slept for the crowd of nightmares, and watched the street through a slit in the curtains, dreading that day, but it didn't come, and gradually they returned to some semblance of a normal life – more normal, indeed, than their life had been before.

Their saltshaker of diamonds had been lost on the ship in Marseilles, but Yazad gave them more. It had always been he who sent them. He also persuaded Esmé to enroll in a small private school not far from her neighborhood, and she began spending her days with other girls. She was shy among them at first, but they were mostly shy and bookish girls themselves, and for the first time in her life, she made friends. She was discovered to be a gifted violinist, surpassing the music teacher's skill, and so a private instructor was engaged for her. She went to tea with the other girls, and to a birthday party. She brought a wrapped gift, ate a slice of cake, and even danced with a boy – but only once. She didn't enjoy the feeling of his hands heavy at her waist. She thought of another touch, a light, furtive one: the way the flower shop boy had held her braid in his hand when he stood behind her in line at the bakery. It seemed like such a long time ago. The memory of it curved Esmé's lips into a secret smile as she stepped abruptly away from her dance partner and retreated.

A few days later she stopped to buy her mother some flowers on the way home from school. The boy was behind the counter and when he saw her come in, he blushed. He was blond and his eyes were blue, but dark like the deep sea, not icy like Druj blue, and he was fair, with long pale lashes and rosy color in his cheeks as if they'd been pinched pink by aunts and grannies until they stayed that way. He stammered when he helped Esmé gather together a bouquet from the buckets of flowers around the shop.

'Cosmos?' he asked her.

She nodded, adding softly, 'And maybe some lilies.'

'A bit of lupine?' he said, holding up a blue spike of blossoms.

They could think of nothing to say but the names of flowers, and it seemed a sort of language of its own. Mums, zinnias, delphinium, a lacy frond of baby's breath.

As she handed him her money, Esmé blurted her name and then bit her lip.

'I'm Tom,' said the boy, blushing anew.

And that was all. Esmé left with her flowers clutched to her chest and her braid swinging in her haste, but by the time she got to the corner, she was smiling. Perhaps, she thought, she would buy her mother flowers again next week.

And she did.

Time passed. Esmé thought often of the ash of ancient souls blowing ever around the world, sifting and mixing with the ash of forest fires and wars and the dust of deserts and pollen and bones. The ache of absence within her eased some with time; she filled it with music and schoolwork and friends, trips to the ballet with her mother, and walks in St. James's Park with Tom.

The first time, he stammered an invitation over a bouquet of orange roses and Esmé's voice was almost a whisper when she said, 'All right,' her eyes fixed on the flower petals. She met him the next morning with her coat buttoned to her chin and they made their way up Birdcage Walk with their hands shoved deep in their pockets, noses red from the cold. They paused a moment to watch the red-coated soldiers strut at Horse Guards Parade.

'I used to want to be one,' admitted Tom. 'I even practiced marching like them. I didn't know they were real soldiers who go to war. I just liked the caps.'

'They kill bears to make those,' said Esmé.

'I know,' he replied, adding quickly, 'I don't want to be one anymore.'

Turning from the soldiers, they made their way into the park. Tom produced some bread from his pocket and they fed the ducks and watched the famous pelicans cruise through the green waters of the lake like a fleet of small ships. They walked side by side and faced ahead, from time to time daring to dart quick glances at each other. Esmé noticed the good line of Tom's jaw, and Tom marveled at the sweet small perfection of Esmé's face, and their furtive glances kept meeting in the middle. They blushed over and over and shoved their fists deeper into their pockets.

'Thank you for coming,' said Tom when they arrived back at Esmé's door, and Esmé tilted her head back to look up at him – she was only as tall as his shoulder – and she gave him a smile, a tiny flash of joy, that promised more such walks were to come.

The ducks at St. James's Park were no starvelings to start, but over the next weeks and months they grew a little fatter and learned to recognize the red-haired girl and the fair-haired boy who came walking shoulder to shoulder on Sundays with their pockets full of bread. The ducks probably didn't notice, but after a few weeks Esmé and Tom were able to meet glances without looking away (though they did not cease to blush), and gradually, to sit facing each other on a favorite bench and talk, even when a pelican named Vaclav decided to nestle between them and sleep.

Tom always brought Esmé a flower. They were hothouse roses at first, and when spring came around, daffodils, and in summer, dahlia blossoms so big she had to hold them with both hands. She was gazing down at one such on a Sunday in July, sitting on their usual bench. The blossom was white with a delicate blush of pink in its center, and she asked, 'What's it called?'

Tom's cheeks went red. The dahlia's name was 'Crazy Love,' and when he'd picked it out that morning in the shop, he'd known Esmé would ask its name – she loved flower names – and he'd imagined himself telling it to her. It would be, he had thought, a way to say the word 'love' to her. But now that the moment had come, his mouth went dry. He mumbled something.

Not understanding, Esmé looked at him and saw his red cheeks, his anxious eyes. 'What?' she asked softly.

He swallowed, and his voice cracked as he repeated, 'It's called Crazy Love,' but he did manage to meet Esmé's eyes for just an instant on the word 'love.'

She looked quickly back down at the blossom's blushing center, and she felt as if that small word was opening her like a bud, like the sun had touched her and she was unfurling her petals to better draw its warmth. She smiled, flushed. Tom saw and, seized by a sudden surge of perfect boldness, he leaned in.

In a dark layer of Esmé's memory there was a kiss. Vividly she recalled Mihai in the snow, naked and fanged. That kiss had conjured ancient passions a god had tried to erase, and Esmé remembered the pressure of it and even knew the flavor of that black river. But it belonged to someone else. Tom's kiss, by contrast, wasn't passionate.

Esmé didn't even have time to close her eyes and tilt her face up to meet it, and it landed crooked and only half on her lips. It was clumsy and it ended quickly.

And it was hers.

Tom sat back and stared down at his hands, mortified by his own daring.

Esmé's heart thudded a few fast beats and then she reached out tentatively and slipped her fingers into his. They held hands all the way back up Birdcage Walk and without discussing it, they took a circuitous path home so they might keep their fingers entwined as long as possible, and then they lingered at Esmé's door, reluctant to let go.

Over time Tom's kisses learned their way to Esmé's lips, but they stayed gentle and he still blushed every time he saw her. Whether he might be the soul mate with whom she would share her centuries remained to be seen. They were only children, as Mab had never been allowed to be, and it was sweet. Esmé was happy, but there was always a sense, like a phantom pain, that she had lost some piece of herself. During quiet moments, sometimes, the loss overwhelmed her as surely as a mother's empty, aching arms.

She turned fifteen, and still Mahzarin did not come.

Mihai became like a ghost. He sat for hours on rooftops and church spires, traveling through visions of an ancient time. Fog swam round his still shape and sometimes rain sluiced down his hair. Birds ignored him and went about their own rooftop lives, sometimes even perching on him for minutes before he realized it and shook them off.

And then came an evening in winter when the sky was starless black and as cold as Druj flesh. He was resting against a stone steeple with his chin on his chest when he felt the riffling draft of wings and then a weight settled on his knee. He jerked his leg to dislodge it, but it only hovered and beat its wings and settled on him again. Mihai lifted his head to look. His eyes widened. It was no pigeon or crow perched on him. It was an eagle, its vast wings half spread, its talons thick as fingers, and its eyes blue and pale as ice. Around its feathered neck hung a moonstone amulet and, tied to that, the last remnant of the persimmon-red braid the Druj Queen had cut from Mab years ago.

Everything in Mihai tensed and clenched and froze, his heartbeat, his breath, his sore and dwindling hope. He just stared at the eagle, and it stared back. A moment passed like that before Mihai's mind unfroze and began to spin. The eagle fanned its wings once more and then folded them.

It was waiting.

It had been more than five hundred years since Mihai had whispered another Druj back to human cithra, but he remembered the words. They caught in his throat as the enormity of the moment choked him. The Queen of the Druj did not shift cithra. Ever. She did not leave her fate and flesh to the whims and whispers of others. This cithra was an offering.

Mihai took a ragged breath and readied himself to voice the ancient words. He lifted his arms. They trembled. Even after all these centuries, his arms remembered the curve of Mahzarin's body, the weight and the warmth of her, and when she shimmered forth from the feathers of her eagle cithra, he would be there to catch her.

My long fascination with the remarkable poem by Christina Rossetti, 'Goblin Market,' has previously resulted in paintings, goblin masks, and – in a roundabout way – a stage adaptation at Stanford University! Now it has flowered into a story that gave me great joy to write. Likewise, my fascination with the British Raj, other cultures' concepts of Hell, and the ancient Persian religion of Zoroastrianism were seeds of inspiration, but only seeds – I am no scholar, and have plundered tidbits of history and lore to build something new, using only the parts that light my mind on fire.

Some readers may wonder why, in 'Spicy Little Curses Such as These,' innocent children and even babies are ending up in Hell. The answer is that, to my understanding, the Hindu concept of Heaven and Hell is not nearly so simple, nor so black and white, as the Judeo-Christian one. I can't begin to try to encompass it, but in my creation I was drawing on the idea that the attainment of Heaven is a very long and rigorous process for a soul, and only accomplished after many, many lifetimes of virtue. The 'Hell' that fits into this cycle of reincarnation is not, here, solely a place of punishment for the wicked, but a place of remaking that everyone, even the innocent, must pass through. Likewise, Yama is not the devil, but a god of judgment, and the Fire is a place of purification.

In the Zoroastrian faith, the word 'druj' signifies the opposite of 'asha,' which is the truth and order of God's creation; 'druj' is chaos and deceit. There is some demon lore associated with Zoroastrianism, but the demonic Druj of 'Hatchling' are entirely my own creation. Pillaging the dead Avestan language to invent Druj-speak was great fun, but if you happen to *speak* said dead language, please forgive the liberties I have taken. Like a magpie, I am a scavenger of shiny things: fairy tales, dead languages, weird folk beliefs, fascinating religions, and more.

· ACKNOWLEDGMENTS ·

Without two particular people, it is highly unlikely this book would exist.

Meg Genge, my fabulous Canadian cohort in Sunday Scribblings. We started a writing-prompt site to get ourselves (and others) writing, and it worked! (All welcome: www.sundayscribblings.blogspot.com)

Jim Di Bartolo, who convinced me these kissing stories could be a book, and whose beautiful art adds a whole new dimension to them. Thank you!

Thanks also to first readers Alexandra Saperstein, Chary Deutsch, and my mom, Patti Taylor, and of course to my wonderful agent Jane Putch, for boundless enthusiasm.

Massive thanks to the folks who really turned these stories into a book: Arthur Levine, whose praise makes me feel like a genius; Rachel Griffiths and Cheryl Klein for liking the manuscript and passing it on to him; Emily Clement for all the things in between; Elizabeth Parisi and Chris Stengel for art and style; and the rest of the team at Arthur A. Levine Books and Scholastic.

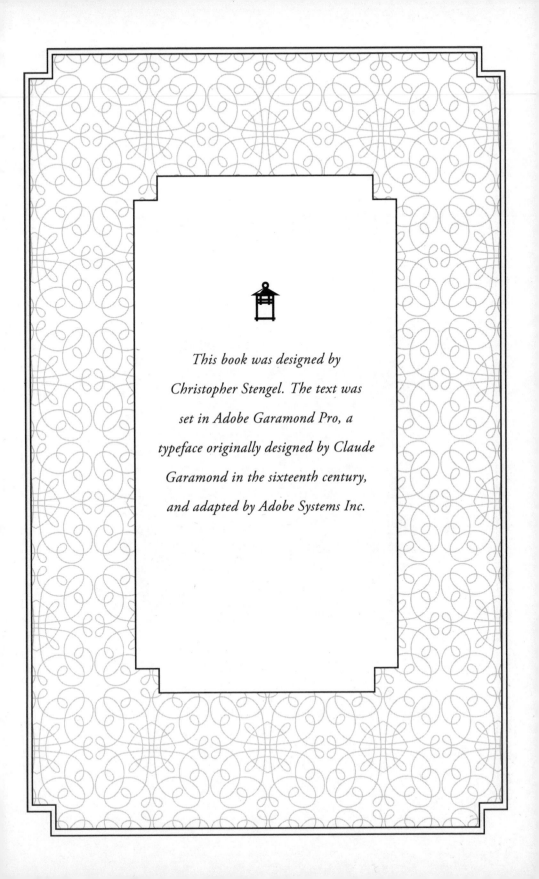

This book was designed by
Christopher Stengel. The text was
set in Adobe Garamond Pro, a
typeface originally designed by Claude
Garamond in the sixteenth century,
and adapted by Adobe Systems Inc.